THE
BIOGRAPHICAL
DICTIONARY
OF
LITERARY
FAILURE

— The —

BIOGRAPHICAL

DICTIONARY

— of —

LITERARY FAILURE

Edited by C. D. ROSE

INTRODUCTION BY ANDREW GALLIX

MELVILLE HOUSE

BROOKLYN — LONDON

The Biographical Dictionary of Literary Failure

First Melville House printing
— NOVEMBER 2014 —

MELVILLE HOUSE PUBLISHING
145 PLYMOUTH STREET
BROOKLYN, NY 11201

— and —

8 BLACKSTOCK MEWS
ISLINGTON
LONDON N4 2BT

mhpbooks.com
facebook.com/mhpbooks
@melvillehouse

ISBN: 978-1-61219-378-6

LIBRARY OF CONGRESS
CATALOGING-IN-PUBLICATION DATA:

Rose, C. D., author.
  The biographical dictionary of literary failure / C. D. Rose ; introduction
by Andrew Gallix.
    pages cm
  ISBN 978-1-61219-378-6 (hardback)
  ISBN 978-1-61219-379-3 (ebook)
  1. Authors—Biography—Dictionaries—Fiction. 2. Failure (Psychology)—
Fiction. I. Title.
  PS3618.O78284B56 2014
  813'.6—dc23

                                                    2014002517

PRINTED IN THE UNITED STATES OF AMERICA
DESIGNED BY SAM POTTS

1 3 5 7 9 10 8 6 4 2

CONTENTS

INTRODUCTION

ONCE upon a time this book was a website celebrating the lives of writers who have 'achieved some measure of literary failure'. Every week a new biography was posted, anonymously, and after a year all the entries were duly deleted, thus enacting their own subject matter. It struck me as a beautiful echo of Maurice Blanchot's oft-quoted prophecy that literature is 'heading toward itself, toward its essence, which is its disappearance.' I also realised that this online compendium, culled from the slush pile of history by C. D. Rose and his team of researchers, was simply too valuable to be allowed to disappear without trace, however romantic the gesture.

The impulse to tell the tales of those whose tales will remain untold is akin to that which inspired the creation of the various libraries of unpublished and unwritten books (often modelled on the library in Richard Brautigan's *The Abortion*). Hannah Arendt once wondered if the very notion of 'unappreciated genius'—the *poète maudit* whose prodigious talent goes unrecognised in his or her lifetime—was not simply 'the daydream of those who are not geniuses.' I suspect that there is indeed a touch of Schadenfreude about the pleasure derived from reading these anecdotes of writerly woe. The cumulative effect produces a kind of *comique de répétition* that takes its cue from Beckett: 'Ever tried. Ever failed. No matter. Try again. Fail again. Fail better.' There is a slight sadistic thrill each time you move on to the next sob story, and try to guess how this hapless scribe will manage to fail even better than the previous one. I also suspect that the editor—who had achieved some measure of literary success, but not, alas, the breakthrough he deserved—may have been exorcising some demons of his own.

Literary biography is a by-product of literature: the writer's life is read, *à rebours*, in the light of her works. Had she not written them, we would probably show no interest in the minutiae of her existence. Literature redeems daily life, endowing it with meaning; recasting it, teleologically, as a prolegomenon to the work. By its very nature, *The Biographical Dictionary of Literary Failure* raises some crucial questions. Literature is all about readers losing themselves in books and writers losing themselves in a language that speaks itself. If, as Roland Barthes argued, the death of the author marks the birth of literature, does the death of literature—its loss, or failure to come into being—mark the rebirth of the author? Is it possible, as Jean-Yves Jouannais believes, to be a writer without writings? 'The writer doesn't really want to write, he wants to be; and in order to truly be, he must face up to the difficult challenge of not writing at all,' states one of Luis Chitarroni's characters in *The No Variations*. Not writing, for a writer, may be writing by another means, or rather the logical conclusion of the literary enterprise, for, as Enrique Vila-Matas highlights, 'in the end, every book pursues non-literature as the essence of what it wants and passionately desires to discover.'

The fifty-two writers manqués whose names are saved from oblivion in this dictionary certainly did not fail through lack of ambition. Quite the contrary. Most of them devoted their lives to the pursuit of some *Gesamtkunstwerk* that was supposed to encompass the whole of being, but resulted in nothingness. This quixotic quest for a volume in which everything would be said extends from epic poetry to Joyce's *Ulysses* through the Bible, the Summa Theologica, Coleridge's omnium-gatherum, the great encyclopedias, Proust's masterpiece, Mallarmé's (non-)conception of 'Le Livre,' and Borges's 'total book'—the 'catalog of catalogs'—rumoured to be lurking on some dusty shelf in the Library of Babel. Take the example of Edward Nash, who was convinced that absolutely everything 'that needed to be written' could be expressed, if only he managed to find the perfect way of describing an individual cloud or wave. He spent most of his days staring at the sea and sky, and most of his nights filling notebooks with odd words and phrases. Never once was he able to complete a single sentence, unlike Chad Sheehan, who, in a flash of inspiration, jotted down the perfect opening to a story. Whenever he attempted to compose the following sentence, however, he ended up with the opening line to another story. This oscillation between totality and fragmentation—already experienced by the Jena romantics, often regarded as the originators of modern literature—is best illustrated by Nate Warronker, who painstakingly planned to write the longest novel in history without ever considering its actual content. Felix Dodge embodies another crucial aspect of literary modernity: the failure to even begin the work, let alone complete it. He spent twenty years limbering up for a magnum opus that would have included 'everything that was or could be known to humanity'—had he not died just as he was about to put pen to paper.

In 1975, Ulises Carrión declared: 'The most beautiful and perfect book in the world is a book with only blank pages.' Such books of 'absolute whiteness' had featured in Eastern legends for centuries—echoed by the blank map in 'The Hunting of the Snark' or the blank scroll in *Kung Fu Panda*— but they only really appeared on bookshelves in the twentieth century. They come in the wake of Bartleby (Melville's scrivener who stops scrivening), Rimbaud's renunciation of poetry and Hofmannsthal's aphasia-afflicted Lord Chandos. They are contemporaneous with the Dada suicides, Wittgenstein's coda to the *Tractatus*, the white paintings of Malevich or Rauschenberg, Yves Klein's vacant exhibitions, as well (of course) as John Cage's mute music piece. Blankness is the sine qua non for inclusion in the *BDLF*, but it is seldom sought after directly. Manuscripts and books remain blank to us through being censored, lost, drowned, shredded, pulped, burned, used as cigarette paper or wrapped around kebabs, fed to pigs or even ingested by their own authors . . . Marta Kupka produces a blank memoir, not of her own volition, but due to a potent combination of failing eyesight and dried-up typewriter ribbon. The closest we get to a genuine hankering after blankness comes from the two erasers included in the book: Virgil Haack, who whittles down his work to a single word (à la François Le Lionnais), and Wendy Wenning, who edits her 'thousand-page epic' until she is left with a 'perfectly blank sheet of paper.' It is suggested that it may be the 'fear of someone actually reading their work' that causes authors like Stanhope Barnes, or T. E. Lawrence before him, to lose their manuscripts at Reading station. I think this comment applies to all the entries. These brief biographies are sketches that merely gesture towards the possibility of narrative development; stories that are cut short or fall silent. Stories that *would prefer not to*.

We learn that Jürgen Kittler aimed to 'rebuild language itself,' just like Stéphane Mallarmé, who set out to 'purify the words of the tribe.' The French fin-de-siècle poet was influenced by Hegel, for whom language negates things and beings in their singularity, replacing them with concepts (as Edward Nash learned to his cost). From then on, literature would be officially at war with itself—language being both medium and enemy: 'A book that does not contain its counterbook is considered incomplete' (Borges). If words give us the world by taking it away, then the solution might be, as Beckett would argue, to 'drill one hole after another' into them 'until that which lurks behind, be it something or nothing, starts seeping through.' The protagonist of Steven Millhauser's recent 'History of a Disturbance'—a latter-day Lord Chandos—vows no longer 'to smear the world with sentences.' He even endeavours to 'erase word-thoughts' in his quest for 'a place where nothing is known, because nothing is shaped in advance by words.' After Balzac, the realist novel had taken on an Adamic quality by colonising the singular and contingent: aspects of experience that had no prior linguistic expression. Logoclasts like Beckett sought to put an end to this literary imperialism through a process of unnaming—the deployment of a self-effacing 'literature of the unword.' In *Molloy*, the narrator draws the radical conclusion that 'all language' is 'an excess of language,' even suggesting that it may be preferable 'to obliterate texts,' to 'fill in the holes of words till all is blank and flat,' rather than 'blacken margins' like an eejit. Here, in the *BDLF*, we are introduced to Aurelio Quattrochi, an enigmatic writer who 'spent all of 1973 poring over a single word, and most of 1974 erasing it.'

Erasure may be one way of exploring a prelinguistic, prelapsarian world untainted by human consciousness; another is to make words so obtrusive that they cease to be transparent and blot out everything else. For the likes of Mallarmé and Blanchot, literature takes linguistic negation one step further than Hegel, by negating both the real thing and its surrogate concept. Words no longer refer primarily to ideas, but to other words; they become present like the things they negated in the first place. According to Donald Barthelme, a book is thus 'an object in the world rather than a text or commentary upon the world.' Blanchot described writing, in similarly physical terms, as 'a bit of bark, a sliver of rock, a fragment of clay in which the reality of the earth continues to exist.'

Post-Romantic literature was a blank canvas that often dreamed of remaining blank, anyway. The emergence of modern literature coincided with a growing linguistic crisis. After the seventeenth century—after Milton—language had ceased to encompass most aspects of experience. There was, as George Steiner put it, a gradual retreat from the word. Mathematics became increasingly untranslatable, post-Impressionist art escaped verbalisation; linguistics and philosophy highlighted the arbitrary nature of signifiers, meaning was corrupted by the mass media . . . Against this backdrop of declining confidence in the powers of language—just as Schiller's 'disenchantment of the world' was becoming ever more apparent, and the writer's legitimacy, in a 'destitute time' (Hölderlin) of absent gods and silent sirens (Kafka), seemed ever more arbitrary—literature came to be considered as an 'absolute.' Writers were called upon to fill the spiritual vacuum left by the secularisation of society: they were deified even as their authority was being defied on all fronts. Walter Benjamin famously described the 'birthplace of the novel'—and hence that of modern literature—as 'the solitary individual': an individual free from tradition, but also one whose sole legitimacy derived from him- or herself, rather than religion or society. As soon as this 'solitary individual' was elevated to the status of *alter deus*, the essential belatedness of human creativity became glaringly obvious. In theory, literature could now be anything the author wanted it to be. The snag, as Kierkegaard observed, is that 'more and more becomes possible' when 'nothing becomes actual.' What Paul Valéry described as the 'demon of possibility' is best illustrated by Robert Musil's unfinished (and probably unfinishable) *The Man Without Qualities*—a restless work which, like its eponymous character, attempts to keep all options open by spurning any fixed identity.

Novels were increasingly haunted by the ideal forms of which they were but imperfect instantiations, every book being 'the death mask of its conception' (Walter Benjamin), 'the wreck of a perfect idea' (Iris Murdoch), the betrayal of all perfection' (David Foster Wallace). Completing a text became a form of capitulation: 'This book is my cowardice,' wrote Fernando Pessoa, who envied the courage of Félicien Marboeuf, the 'greatest writer never to have written.' The latter entertained such a lofty conception of literature that any novels he may have perpetrated could only have been pale reflections of their sublime inspiration. (A young Proust gushed that every single page he had failed to write had achieved perfection.) Literature, in other words, was now programmed to fail. Karl Ove Knausgaard defines writing as 'failing with total dedication.' Tom McCarthy claims that literature is 'always premised on its own impossibility.' Kafka even went as far as to say that the 'essential impossibility of writing' is the 'only thing one can write about.' Or not. Some took refuge in silence; others in destruction. The Baron of Teive (one of Pessoa's numerous heteronyms) tops himself after destroying most of his manuscripts due to the impossibility of producing 'superior art.' In Dadaist circles, suicide even came to be seen as a form of inverted transcendence, a rejection of the reality principle and an antidote to literary mystification. 'You're just a bunch of poets and I'm on the side of death' was Jacques Rigaut's parting shot to the Surrealists. Like him, Arthur Cravan, Jacques Vaché, Boris Poplavsky, Julien Torma, Danilo Kupus and René Crevel all chose to make the ultimate artistic statement.

Michael Gibbs, who published an anthology of blank books entitled *All or Nothing*, points out that going to all the trouble of producing such workless works 'testifies to a faith in the ineffable.' This very same faith prompts Borges to claim that 'for a book to exist, it is sufficient that it be *possible*.' Marcel Bénabou argues that the books he has failed to write are not 'pure nothingness': they exist, virtually, in some Borgesian library of phantom fictions. This is also what George Steiner means when he states, 'A book unwritten is more than a void.'

For Blanchot, the impossibility of ever producing a complete work—a materialisation of the Absolute in book form—preserves literature as *possibility*. He described Joseph Joubert as 'one of the first entirely modern writers' because the latter saw literature as the 'locus of a secret that should be preferred to the glory of making books.' Cioran attacked Mallarmé for the very same reason: 'If Mallarmé intrigues us, it is because he fulfills the conditions of the writer who is unrealised in relation to the disproportionate ideal he has assigned himself . . . We are adepts of the work that is aborted, abandoned halfway through, impossible to complete, undermined by its very requirements.' Modernity, as Steiner also points out, 'often prefers the sketch to the finished painting and prizes the draft, chaotic with corrections, to the published text.' Like Joubert and Mallarmé, Roland Barthes was more interested in 'sacrificing results to the discovery of their conditions.' At the outset of his series of lectures entitled *The Preparation of the Novel*, he announces his intention to proceed '*as if*' he were going to write a novel: 'It's therefore possible that the Novel will remain at the level of—or be exhausted by—its Preparation.' In his famous foreword to *The Garden of Forking Paths*, Borges had advocated a similar approach: 'It is a laborious madness and an impoverishing one, the madness of composing vast books—setting out in five hundred pages an idea that can be perfectly related orally in five minutes. The better way to go about it is to pretend that those books already exist, and offer a summary, a commentary on them.' Blaise Cendrars thus toyed with the idea of a bibliography of unwritten works. In his debut, Edouard Levé gave brief descriptions of more than 500 books he had envisaged but never actually written. Enrique Vila-Matas's *Bartleby & Co.* is a series of footnotes on an 'invisible' text. Both Geoff Dyer's *Out of Sheer Rage* and Jacques Roubaud's *The Great Fire of London* are books about the failure to write a book. Ivan Vladislavić's *The Loss Library* is a reflexion upon stories the author had 'imagined but could not write, or started to write but could not finish.' Luis Chitarroni's *The No Variations* is a series of aborted notes for an aborted novel. Nick Thurston's *Reading the Remove of Literature* is an edition of *The Remove of Literature* from which Blanchot's original text has been erased, leaving only the author's marginalia . . .

Writing *about* fictitious or lost works is a means of holding literature in abeyance, of preserving its potentiality. In a way, *The Biographical Dictionary of Literary Failure* is and is not. Yes, you are holding a copy in your hands, and yes, it contains fifty-two reasons why this is a small miracle; yet it is still a *book to come.*

THE
BIOGRAPHICAL
DICTIONARY
OF
LITERARY
FAILURE

CASIMIR
ADAMOWITZ-KOSTROWICKI

THINK, IF YOU WILL, of Kafka asking Max Brod and Dora Diamant to burn all his papers when he eventually succumbed to the TB that had been slowly killing him for years. Think of Virgil, weak with fever and unable to put the finishing marks on his *Aeneid*, arriving in the harbour at Brindisi and asking that his work be destroyed rather than left unfinished. Think of Lavinia Dickinson, who did not burn her sister's poems. And now think of Casimir Adamowitz-Kostrowicki.

You cannot, of course, because unlike Franz Kafka, Publius Vergilius Maro and Emily Dickinson, Casimir Adamowitz-Kostrowicki had a friend faithless enough to obey his dying wishes.

We cannot think of Adamowitz-Kostrowicki because we know nothing of him, but imagine if Kafka's best friend and his lover had done what was bid of them, if Virgil's scribes hadn't had the emperor Augustus telling them what not to do and if Lavinia had not been so wily in interpreting her sister's will and burned the poems as well as the letters, which she did destroy.

This, too, is almost impossible, as you are being asked to imagine what is *not*, rather than what could have been. Imagine a void; imagine blankness. Imagine a literary world—or, indeed, *any* world—which has not in some sense been shaped by Kafka's dark fables, Virgil's Roman epic and Dickinson's poetic invention. We cannot know, of course, but it is possible that Adamowitz-Kostrowicki's work would have had a comparable influence on the way we interpret the world around us.

Casimir Adamowitz-Kostrowicki was born to a Polish father and American mother in Paris in 1880, initially trained to be a chemist but was soon distracted by the emergent technologies of film, photography and sound recording. These pursuits led him to frequent more bohemian circles and attempt to record and portray some of the people he admired most: Picasso and Apollinaire, Rilke and Lou Andreas-Salomé, Ezra Pound, Wyndham Lewis and the young T. S. Eliot.

Inspired by their example, Adamowitz-Kostrowicki began to write and showed his work to many of his subjects, who all responded with enthusiasm. However, he refused to allow anything to be published, claiming his greatest work was yet to be completed. In 1914, he volunteered, joined a French artillery battalion and left a suitcase containing all of his writings with his closest friend, Eric Levallois. Adamowitz-Kostrowicki firmly instructed his friend that were he not to return, Levallois should destroy the entire contents of the case, including his magnum opus—the first great modern novel—*L'homme avec les mains fleuries*. This, it is said, was a work which would have overshadowed *La Recherche*, made *The Man Without Qualities* look as dull as its title, dwarf *Ulysses* in its range and scope, render *To the Lighthouse* small and parochial.

By 1918, Levallois had not heard a word from his friend and, desolate, built a small bonfire on the street outside his Montmartre home. Passers-by thought he was celebrating the end of the war.

(Unknown to Levallois, Adamowitz-Kostrowicki had not perished at the front but had been badly shellshocked and did indeed return to Paris that very week, and may have even been trying to visit his friend, but a horse, spooked by fireworks set off as part of the festivities, bolted and trampled him to death.)

So think again of Kafka and Virgil and Dickinson, and think of how we cannot know what has been lost, not only from an unfortunate like Adamowitz-Kostrowicki, but from those dozens or hundreds or thousands whose work has been lost to fire or flood, to early death, to loss, to theft or to the censor's pyre. What has been lost that could have bettered us all?

STANHOPE BARNES

COMPARED TO THAT OF Casimir Adamowitz-Kostrowicki,* the case of Stanhope Barnes may seem significantly more prosaic. For Barnes there was no deathbed insistence, no last testament, no relative or friend placed in an agonising moral quandary. His work did not, as far as we know, go through the teeth of a cruelly ironic shredding machine or meet any bitter flames. No, Stanhope Barnes merely made the mistake—in an age long before flash drives, memory sticks, Dropbox or the iCloud—of leaving the only manuscript of his work on a train.

---

* See entry no. 1.

At first, this seems like a poor example of failure. This man, you may think, was no great artist manqué frustrated by cruel fate, but a mere fool. We at the *BDLF*, however, beg to differ. Stanhope Barnes was far from being a fool, and what was left on that threadbare second-class seat at Reading station may have been the equivalent of *The Trial* or *The Aeneid* or 'Because I could not stop for death.'

Born into a working-class family in Nottinghamshire in 1897, Barnes was part of a generation shaped by their experiences on the battlefields of the Somme, experiences which he would fashion into *Here Are the Young Men*, the novel lost on the train as he was taking it to London to discuss its publication with T. S. Eliot at Faber and Faber. The book was a modernist epic which would have changed the perception of First World War writers as doomed poets, and place them squarely in the modern forge. *Here Are the Young Men* was a deeply felt work about the horrors of the war on a par with *In Parenthesis* or *Mrs Dalloway*. Its loss is incalculable.

And though the circumstances surrounding this loss may seem foolish, how much more closely does this touch our own experience? Few of us have ever had to make a life-or-death decision, but many of us—whether on buses or trains or in bars or restaurants—will have lost valued objects through hurry, stress or sheer neglect. (Freud, of course, would claim this means we wish to return to the scene of the loss, that we are re-enacting some primal grievance, and though we are baffled as to why Barnes may have wished to return to Reading, we cannot help but note that T. E. Lawrence also famously left the first draft of *The Seven Pillars of Wisdom* in the same place. Is there, we wonder, some association with that dull junction's homonym, that it is a writer's fear of someone actually reading their work that causes these slips?)

We are left only to wonder: what happened to that manuscript? There are stories: that it was discovered by an avid reader who loved it so much he locked it in a vault or hid it in an attic to be discovered by an as yet unarrived posterity; that it was found by a kindly stranger who spoke no English but took it to home to Paraguay and had it translated into Spanish, where, by dint of an extremely poor translation it became known as *¿Dónde están los jóvenes?*, a hugely successful account of a youth football team touring war-torn Europe and succumbing to random sniper fire (even forming the basis for a 1970s *telenovela*); that it met the requirements of another poor traveller stranded in the Thames Valley in urgent need of toilet paper. But these stories are only hearsay, and have yet to be proved.

In his novel *The Angel of History*, Bruno Arpaia suggests that Walter Benjamin's last lost work was entrusted to an anti-Franco fighter who used it to light a fire and consequently save himself from freezing to death on a Pyrenean mountainside when fleeing from persecution. We can only hope Stanhope Barnes's work may, in its last moments, have saved a life.

THE BEASLEY COLLECTIVE

FEW GREAT LITERARY WORKS have ever been composed by more than one hand. While some early poems (including the *Odyssey* and the *Mahabharata*) may well have been the product of several authors over long periods of time, the modern age has nothing comparable. The *Preface to the Lyrical Ballads* was quite obviously the work of Wordsworth, however he and Coleridge may have pretended. Auden and Isherwood collaborated briefly, but without fireworks. The *Groep 52* experimented in the Netherlands, while in Italy Luther Blissett and various Wu Mings have pointed the way but inevitably fell into solipsistic fragmentation. A number of genre writers are more or less committees, but have produced little that will last.

What is it about the group or collective that so proscribes literary greatness? There may be many answers to this question, but the most significant is probably the brute fact that writing remains an intensely solitary activity.

Some, however, persuaded either by recognition of their own lack or more often, it seems, by ideological reasons, have tried to buck this trend. One such group would be the Beasley Collective.

Formed in Hulme, Manchester, in 1979 (and not, in fact, named after the John Cooper Clarke poem, but after the location of the communal squat where they all resided), the Collective wanted to take the ideological drive of the post-punk era and marry it to the sheer thrill of being in a band, but seeing as none of them could play instruments (not, it has to be said, a barrier that stopped many in that fertile time) decided to work in the literary sphere. They could all read and write, after all. Such a strategy would, they believed 'attack imperialist high culture from the inside.'

While most were anarchists, others were Maoists, Trotskyites, anarcho-syndicalists, Leninists, Marxist-Leninists, Kropotkinites and radical Lacanians. Jürgen Kittler* was briefly, it is said, a member, probably during his stint as bass player with the semi-legendary band King Ink.

The Collective liberated an IBM Selectric from the insurance agency where one of them worked by day, and established a rigorous compositional method. They would sit in a circle on the floor of their sparsely furnished house

* See entry no. 20.

and in turn type one word each, slowly stringing together the sentences of literary works which, they hoped, would blow apart the postwar neoliberal consensus.

Their first work was, of course, a manifesto.

There is no literary form more thrilling than the manifesto. To emblazon ideas across the artistic firmament or make a grand declaration in the belief that what one is doing will change human society without, yet, actually having to bother doing anything that will make such proclamations true is an exciting endeavour.

Only one copy of the *Beasley Collective Manifesto* was ever produced: the Xerox machine at the insurance agency was due for servicing.

Undeterred, the Collective carried on composing, though their rigorous method meant that works were slow in coming. Each word typed was given over to strict ideological analysis and heated debate. It took them six months to produce their first short story, but then it was decided that the short story was a commercial form and not applicable to their radical standards. Further discussion saw the novel deemed 'bourgeois' and poetry 'elitist.'

Most bands split up due to musical differences (usually a shorthand for the simple fact they can't stand each other anymore), most writers keep on going, producing ever-inferior work or giving up when they have nothing left to say. The Beasley Collective was, at least, unique in this perspective: their work ceased in 1982 due to 'ideological incompatibility.' For this, at least, they deserve to be remembered here.

ERNST BELLMER

'EVERYONE HAS A BOOK inside them,' it is often said, and while this may or may not be true, for Ernst Bellmer the commonplace had an unusual validity.

Born in Vienna in 1875, Bellmer grew up the autodidact son of an innkeeper, voraciously reading anything that was left lying around in his father's hostelry. Feuilletons and three-decker novels, penny dreadfuls and pages of the yellow press, chapbooks, almanacs, encyclopedias and broadsides: all were devoured by his gaze. By the age of eighteen, he had ingested enough to begin producing. Over the course of the next few years, Bellmer wrote at least fifty tales (mostly closely observed vignettes of lower-middle-class Viennese life) as well as an epic bildungs-roman, *Der mann mit den blühenden händen*, concerning the life of a lower-middle-class Viennese innkeeper's son and his desperate struggle to become an artist.

But Bellmer was vexed, and it was not the sad failure to find a publisher for his many writings that vexed him. Bellmer suffered, but not from that familiar graphomane pull, that need to translate every thought, feeling or event of his life into words, that overwhelming desire to record and memorise everything by folding it into a more or less probable narrative. No, Bellmer had a less familiar problem: he was a bibliophage. For Bellmer, the aesthetic act was not complete unless his words, once committed to paper, were then eaten.

Bibliophagy is a rare complaint, its very existence doubted by many clinical practitioners and often used as a metaphor rather than in its strict pathological sense. Yet to Bellmer, who suffered not only from this strange psychological compulsion but also from the crippling indigestion it engendered, it was very real.

One of his father's regular clients made him an appointment with Wilhelm Fliess, but the doctor found Bellmer's condition insufficiently interesting (or, perhaps, insufficiently lucrative) and passed it on to his friend and colleague Sigmund Freud (who included a study of the case, entitled 'The Book Eater,' in an early version of *Three Essays on the Theory of Sexuality*, only to have it removed by his editors who doubted its veracity). Freud in turn passed Bellmer on to Friedrich Loeb (grandfather of Max-well*), with whom he sustained a long-lasting though ultimately unsuccessful analysis. He died at the age of seventy-five from ink poisoning.

It seems sad that Bellmer's undoubtedly fascinating excavations of the underbelly of fin-de-siècle Viennese life will never be read, and more intrepid researchers may well have dived into the Austrian capital's sewers to find what remains of his manuscripts, but there we shall not go, leaving Bellmer's work to decay (as surely as all books one day shall).

---

* See entry no. 23.

THOMAS BODHAM

MEN LIKE THOMAS BODHAM are rare these days. Born into an impoverished family in the eponymous Norfolk village in 1720, Thomas knew he was destined to be a traveller when at the age of two the family's only book, *The Pilgrim's Progress*, fell from a high shelf onto his head. He was too young to remember the incident, but the story was often told when Thomas asked about the large indentation it had left on his prominent forehead. With the aid of the kindly pastor's Sunday school lessons, Thomas taught himself to read, practising his skills on the family's only resource until his father swapped the book for a pig during the particularly harsh winter of 1732. The pig died soon after, and Thomas was allowed only its foot to eat.

The book had fed his thirst for adventure, as books are wont to do, and like many young men from his village Bodham took to sea as soon as he was able, seeing the flat fields around him as scant fertiliser for his questing mind. Moreover, he had never forgiven his father for his act of philistinism, nor less for the meagre trotter. As an act of small revenge, he took the family's only remaining treasure, a pair of silver buckles (bequeathed to the Bodhams, so family lore had it, by King Charles himself) on his travels, believing they would keep him fortunate and safe.

Some years later, marooned in Goa by a treacherous Portuguese merchant, Thomas found himself no longer able to stand the permanent seasickness he had endured since he had first set foot on a ship in Great Yarmouth, nor the mariner's continuous diet of salt cod and pickled cabbage. While he still longed for the adventure that had so far failed to present itself to him, he realized he missed those flat, open fields and wishing he could eat a jellied pork by-product. He therefore decided to find his Wicket Gate, House Beautiful and Delectable Mountains by making his way from the western shores of the great subcontinent all the way back to Norfolk on foot.

It was as he set forth that he decided to record the tales of the adventures he would have, encouraged to write like so many by a fear of forgetting and a desire to prove that his fantastic voyages had genuinely taken place. And so, armed with a quire of parchment, squid ink and any writing implement he could lay his hands on, he began to

compose his great tale, *The Lyffe and Travells of Thos. Bodham, Esq.*

Space prevents us from recounting his amazing adventures, and in truth we can only be certain of their end.
We must rely on hearsay and historical footnotes for his
accounts of Jerusalem, Damascus, Istanbul, Byzhzh and
remote cities in Russia, of tribesmen and goatherds, pa-
shas and palaces, for the only thing we know for sure is
that having crossed the Bosphorus and reaching the gates
of Vienna, Bodham was approached by a merchant who
claimed that a published version of his great work would
surely make him a fortune. Bodham, by now penniless and
gaunt, was taken in by the man's tale and handed over his
great manuscript (now amounting to more than a thousand pages). No sooner had he done so when the merchant
slid a thin blade between Bodham's skinny ribs, killing the
weakened traveller instantly.

The merchant, having no genuine interest in what he
believed to be a poorly written ragbag of fibs and outrages,
fed the manuscript to his pigs, removed the shiny silver
buckles from the traveller's worn shoes and then disposed
of the body in the same way he had disposed of the pages
of fascination and wonder that had made Bodham's life.

Bodham's story is an epic writ small, but no less epic
for that. Were he alive today, Thomas Bodham may have
chosen to recount his experiences as a blog or a trail of
Facebook updates. We wonder, in genuine perplexity, why
we feel such an account would have been so much less.

ASTON BROCK

WRITING IS ONE of the lowest paid artistic vocations. In the very rare occasions that a writer manages to make a half-decent sum, the press go apoplectic, as if anybody could do such a thing.

This situation becomes especially pronounced when comparing the most successful writers with the most successful of their colleagues in the visual arts. Even an IMPAC-nominated Booker-winning MacArthur genius cannot hope to command the eye-watering sums raised at auction by Hirst, Richter or Twombly.

The reasons for this are many and beyond the scope of this humble record, though one significant factor is surely the work of art's uniqueness: its aura as a singular object.

It was with this in mind that Aston Brock decided, seeing as his attempts to break into literary renown had yet been unsuccessful, that he would henceforth publish his work in limited editions of one. One copy, only. No more, ever. The author's signature would grace the title page.

Thus, reasoned Aston (a fifty-four-year-old economics graduate whose only venture into the world of hedge funds had seen him lose billions on investments in video discs, virtual reality headsets and futures on the Greek drachma, consequently leading banks worldwide to cancel any trace of his existence), his novel *Christ versus Warhol* would attain the status and price tag of such works of art as Jasper Johns's *Gray Numbers* ($40 million), Gerhard Richter's *Three Candles* ($8.9 million), Cy Twombly's *Untitled 1970* ($7.6 million) or even Jeff Koons's *Balloon Dog* (a relatively modest $5 million).

Brock paid a modish graphic design company to do the jacket, had it handsomely quarter-bound in Gray 31 Harmatam fine leather and Atlantic Calm cloth sides with a coloured top, magenta and indigo head and tail bands, Fedrigoni Merida endpapers and housed in a watered slipcase, then used his connections in the art worlds of Paris, New York, Munich and Milan to have it put up for auction at Christie's.

It failed to sell, not even for its reserve price. An informal offer of three euro fifty was made, but only on the condition that the buyer could have it in e-book format.

Brock, perhaps unsurprisingly, declined the offer, and the single copy of *Christ versus Warhol* currently lies under his bed.

We do not berate Aston Brock for his presumption; we admire him for his courage. We do not pass judgement on a work that, sadly, we have not been able to read, we only offer up his tale as part of our ongoing perplexity about the status of writing in a world which increasingly prefers to look, and not to read.

MARTIN BURSCOUGH

ALL WRITERS' CAREERS, it is said, end in failure. Pity, then, poet Martin Burscough, whose career began in failure.

Burscough, who had passed a long and unspectacular life in financial services, was touched by the muse at a relatively late age when, one afternoon, 'Poetry Please' quietly leaking from the radio on his kitchen windowsill, he saw a one-footed pigeon limping across his back lawn. This strange conjunction hurt him into poetry (as Auden may have put it), resulting in his first ever poem, 'The Pigeon.'

He scribbled the words longhand then dusted off his once-proud Brother AX15 and carefully typed. So pleased by the results, he recalled his favourite bird and wrote 'The Mallard' ('O! Thou green-headed monarch / Of the river-bank . . .'), then 'The Sparrow' and 'The Seagull.' Having exhausted the stock of birds he knew, he headed to his local library to consult an *Observer's* book, and there saw an advertisement for a meeting of his local writers' circle.

A week later he arrived at the meeting only to find the complimentary tea and biscuits already finished ('Nothing but a few crumbs / Left on an empty plate . . .' began the poem he composed to commemorate the occasion). The only person left in the building (not a fellow poet but a librarian) gave Burscough the sad news that due to declining interest, the circle was disbanding. However, she pointed him in the direction of a pile of leaflets, flyers and badly photocopied A4 posters, telling him of the several other poetry events in the area.

The die was cast. Burscough picked up a handful of indicators and began his travels. He mistimed the bus for his first open mike night but harried the flustered organiser nonetheless, only to end up bottom of the list. 'Next time . . .' she told him. For his second attempt, unforeseen circumstances meant the 6:38 from Bodham was cancelled and again he arrived to find a pack of poets departing for the pub, not inviting him along. The third time it was a points failure; on the fourth, a replacement bus service conspired to make him late.

He began to venture farther afield, seeking gatherings of versifiers of any stripe, but found a senior citizens' travel-pass and a mobility scooter unsuited to the demands of the modern professional poet. His routes became more complex and obscure, and from Timperley to Tal-y-Bont, Yate to Yelverton and Ormskirk to Ottery St. Mary, Burscough found Arriva, Greater Anglia, Stagecoach, Plusbus, Onetrains, National Express and Transport for London thwarting him at every turn.

He went to the Hay-on-Wye festival, only to find a wet field filled with abandoned tents and empty wine bottles, then to something calling itself the 'smallest poetry festival in the world.' On arriving, he could not dispute its claim, as he was both the sole poet and the sole audience member.

So if you are ever in Britain, and you use public transport, keep an eye out for a man with a flask of tea and a soggy banana, clutching a Tesco plastic bag filled with typed manuscripts, anxiously checking his watch and a timetable, and admire him.

FELIX DODGE

IT IS OFTEN SAID that a weakness of many first novels is that their over-eager authors cram too much into their pages, fearing they may never write another book again.

This was not, however, entirely the reason that Felix Dodge's debut *The Hourglass* never saw the light of a bookshop or library shelf. Dodge's great worry, contrastingly, was that he would not be able to cram enough into its pages.

Felix Dodge was one of those men fortuitous enough to have been born towards the end of the nineteenth century, in a well-to-do upper-middle-class household in London. An earnest young man, he had little interest in books but had, by the age of eighteen, managed to amass enormous collections of stamps, butterflies, fossils, typewriters, postcards of European spa towns, eighteenth-century Venetian erotica, prize pig rosettes, Palaeolithic axe heads and early modern darning implements. His wide-ranging interests and unbounded curiosity led him to study classics at Cambridge (the only suggestion his baffled schoolmasters could find for him), where, in the second year of his studies, he came upon those twin keystones of High Modernism, *The Waste Land* and a smuggled copy of *Ulysses*, wrapped in sheets of vinegar paper.

Their effect was like a lightning strike for the impressionable young Dodge. Such attempts to encompass almost everything that was knowable (however much their authors may have averred this inference) led him to investigate the idea of the *Gesamtkunstwerk*, a notion that appealed to him greatly, and thus attempt to create his own literary work, one which would include everything that was or could be known to humanity.

Over the next twenty years, Dodge, aided by a small inheritance, squirreled himself away in the great libraries of Europe and North America, undertook ethnographical adventures in the Near, Middle and Far East, travelled to South America in search of the rare *florentibus manu* fungus, to Siberia to map little-known rivers and to Africa to collect creation myths from goat-herding tribes no white man had yet encountered.

His book, he believed, would embrace and obscure the

Kalevala, the Mahabarata, the Bible, the Koran, *The Divine Comedy* and the complete works of Shakespeare, Goethe and all the great Russians. It would make *Moby-Dick* look like a short story, *Finnegans Wake* a mere pamphlet. Among many other things, Dodge investigated and wrote extensive notes on Russian steamships, First World War artillery battalions, the Mauve February anarchists, Old Norse and Anglo-Saxon poetry, the United Kingdom's lesser-used train routes, rare psychological complaints (bibliophagy and graphomania in particular), translations of obscure German and Russian literature, the nature of the true Ark, seventeenth-century traveller's tales, Muscovite street slang, early submarines, Bothno-Ugaric languages, the practice of demonology in West Yorkshire, Age of Discovery–era Portuguese statuary and the contents of the great lost library of Alexandria.

It was only as the Second World War was unleashing its tide of barbarism across Europe that Felix Dodge began to worry. Rightly fearing the destruction of so much knowledge, Felix realised he had lost his narrative thread and, urged by the straitened tenor of the times, knew he had to stop researching and begin writing.

When he discovered that the mere *plan* for his novel ran to over a thousand pages, he seemed to hit upon the idea of concentrating everything he knew into one single story. This, he believed, would expound everything he wished to share.

He put a sheet of paper into his Remington Streamliner and started to type: *The Hourglass*. Enticing as it is, this undoubtedly profound metaphor he had hit upon, the single image which could hold all his thought, was never untied, because, as he finally began to hit the keys in the calm of his Cambridge rooms, surrounded by the thousands of volumes of research he had built up, before his typewriter could even begin to glean his teeming brain, he was struck by a sudden, fatal aneurysm.

Was it, we wonder, the weight of all he knew that caused his grey matter to malfunction so spectacularly, and so tragically?

DANIEL FINNEGAN

WHILE THE *BDLF* is reluctant to dip its toes into the murky waters of contemporary publishing, a recent case has been brought to our attention which, we believe, merits observation.

At first glance, Daniel Finnegan would seem a poor contender for inclusion in these pages. A successful Cambridge graduate, he followed the contemporary career path for an aspirant writer by completing a master's degree in creative writing at one of the more esteemed institutions for such courses, and (unlike many of his classmates) found himself both talented and fortunate enough to emerge from the programme with an agent and, shortly thereafter, a tidy deal with a major publishing conglomerate.

Daniel's novel, *A Breakfast of Thistles*, a delicately observed and finely wrought double narrative recounting the contrasting and interlocking narratives of a nineteenth-century Irish labourer in London and the (semi-autobiographical) tale of a bright young Irishman coming up to Cambridge in the present day, had gained high marks from his supervisors and was initially greeted with enthusiasm by all at his new publishers.

Daniel felt flush with pride, enthusiasm and a handsome (well, handsome enough for these straitened times) advance.

His first doubts came when, over lunch, an editor suggested that he change the navvy into a washerwoman working in large aristocratic household. 'Female migrant narratives are hot at the moment,' she told him, 'and we've got the *Downton* factor in there too. It's win-win.' Persuaded by her forceful manner, Daniel swallowed his objections and produced a new draft.

Six months later, he received a call.

'Hi, Dan!' the voice said.

'It's Daniel.'

'Okay—good and bad news: it's not running well with focus groups,' the assistant editor blandly informed him. 'So we had a brainstorming session, and came up with this: instead of a sensitive poet-type washerwoman, we're thinking of a reality TV contestant. It'll say a lot about, you know, contemporary issues . . .'

Again, Daniel felt he had no choice and duly worked up another draft.

Six months passed, another call. This time it was an intern.

'Hi, Danny!'

'Daniel.'

'Sure. Listen, we're really impressed by the way you've taken on the scathing satire and female subject matter. You *owned* this stuff! You delivered!'

'Thanks.'

'But looking at the whole caboodle, we think it would play better in key secondary markets if the author were a woman.'

Daniel briefly considered the existence of Daniela Finnegan.

'I could give it a try . . .'

'L-O-L! But no need to worry about drag rags just yet. We've found someone else who'll do it.'

'Do what?'

'Oh, cover photo. Title page, that kind of thing. She's a hottie, too—more Irish-looking than you. Red hair, the lot. She interviews well, too. We felt you were a bit, erm, *introspective*. And that's not a criticism! No way! We like introspection, in its place. But, thing is, Dan, we're vision-ing this not so much a book as a marketing campaign. Still there, Dan? Look at this way: now we'll get a crack at the women-only prizes, too!'

'But . . . what about *my book*?'

'No worries, mate. We've listened to what you're saying and we'll take it on board. We'll make sure you get a mention in the acknowledgements.'

Mutely, Daniel hung up the phone.

A year later, via Twitter, Daniel heard the book (*A Breakfast of Bolly*) had won an award for its marketing strategy.

Daniel Finnegan still writes quietly introspective works flecked with dazzle and wonder which no one will ever read.

He has a pocket full of money, but he feels strangely empty.

ELLERY FORTESCUE

WRITING AND ILLNESS make common bedfellows. Keats, a doctor, was constantly coughing, Charlotte Brontë claimed to suffer from fits of hypochondria, Joyce and Beckett sat together for hours comparing maladies real and imagined, and don't even get us started on Marcel Proust.

We do not know if there is some innate link between the two, or if it is the mere fact that writers tend be great self-examiners (or, as the less charitable may call them, narcissists). Were, however, it found to be true, there would hardly be any surprise in the fact: spending many hours sitting alone in poorly heated rooms, seeing little daylight, building up levels of anxiety about the correct deployment of a semi-colon or whether to risk using an adverb is not going to be good for anyone's health, without even thinking about the common attendant vices of alcohol, tobacco or worse. (Here the *BDLF* hastens to recognise that, on a global scale, writing is nowhere near as bad for the health as working in an asbestos factory or cobalt mine.)

Poet and essayist Ellery Fortescue was possessed by doubts about her health. A sickly child, she had resorted to the world of books early on in life, a habit she kept as she grew older, eventually attempting to contribute to their number with her verses and journals, all dedicated to Susan Sontag and the subject of her many ailments. (Often it was nothing greater than a cold that assailed her, but it was all material.)

As she grew older, her illnesses became ever more plural. By the age of twenty-eight, she found herself beset by alternating insomnia and narcolepsy, mysterious weight loss followed by baffling weight gain, aches, pains, blotchy skin, hair loss (head), hair growth (other parts of the body), a constantly running nose, bones that seemed to fracture and ligaments that sprained whenever she tried to hit so much as a single key on her IBM Wheelwriter 3500.

She began to visit doctors, physicians and outright quacks of all persuasions, conventional and complementary, but found them to little effect, until one suggested she try writing therapy.

'Keep a journal,' said the friendly GP. 'Write it all down. It might help.'

'That's what I've been doing all my life,' she replied, but by then the doctor was on to his next patient.

For the next few years, Fortescue listed all her symptoms and feelings about them in an ever-growing pile of notebooks, often wondering what kind of book she could fashion from all this material once it was completed, that is, once she was well again.

Yet that day never seemed to come; the more she wrote, the more sickly she became.

It was only when the pile of notebooks had begun to block the door to her bedroom that she realised she could diagnose herself. She knew what her disease was, and its name: graphomania.

For Fortescue, writing was not a therapy or a cure, but a symptom.

She got out of bed and one by one tore her notebooks up and slowly fed them, leaf by leaf, into her paper shredder. She gave the Wheelwriter (long since without a cartridge) to a local charity shop. She banished any kind of writing implement from her flat.

She has never felt better since.

LAMOTTE FOUQUET

WHAT ARE WE READING when we read a translation? Whatever it may be, a translation is far from being the pure, unmediated word of the book's original author, however much the reader may wish it to be so. Take Nabokov's translation of Lermontov's *A Hero of Our Time*, for example. In a polemical introduction and a series of footnotes no less entertaining than the text itself (the footnotes alone run to some fifteen pages and constantly interrupt the story), Nabokov takes issue with all of the book's previous translators, informs us of the condition of Jewry in early nineteenth-century Caucasus, tells us about honey production and the several different types of alcoholic beverages available in the region, gives us a short essay on the difference between the white acacia and the American black locust tree, tells a history of the publishing record and reception of the works of Byron in Russia and takes a number of vitriolic sideswipes at Honoré de Balzac as well as keeping a running commentary on the text itself (not unoccasionally telling us when he thinks it is rubbish).

Without translation, however, it goes without saying that we would all be much poorer. Anglophones would have no Bolaño, Borges, Calvino, Kharms or Gogol. Readers of other languages would have little Joyce. Yet the act of translating is fraught with pitfalls.

Take, for example, the case of LaMotte Fouquet (1908– 1992; not to be confused with Baron Friedrich La Motte Fouqué, the nineteenth-century German Romantic writer). Despite his name, he was actually English, but born into a polyglot household (his mother Swedish, his father Franco-Polish, his brother Armenian), which meant he spoke eight languages fluently by the age of five, if you do not count his reasonable understanding of Sanskrit.

His father had amassed a fortune in the manufacture of perfumed envelopes, so Fouquet grew up both bookish and entrepreneurial, spending most of his days avoiding school by hiding in the family's vast library. Here, he discovered many great books, both known and unknown, successful and less so. Even as a teenager he dreamed of bringing such works as *The Christ of the Cornfields* (a long handwritten manuscript in Russian, which his father had acquired in exchange for a bottle of plum brandy from some Kazak merchants), *Here Are the Young Men* (a typed draft bought from a house clearance in Reading), *Murderer's Wink* (an agreeable if heavily stained piece of pulp he had found hidden under his mother's bed) or, later, an epic beat poem *In the Scarlet Bathtub* to a wider readership. He eventually decided that a little-known short story entitled 'The Widow's Legs' (by one Ivan Yevachev, of whom LaMotte could find no information at all*) was the tale upon which to practise his genius.

Having read and reread the story several dozen times, he sat down with a Russian dictionary (in truth, superfluous) and began to compose his own version of it. The more he got to grips with the text, however, the more he realised why, perhaps, the story had been so neglected. On closer inspection (and translating a text necessitates very close inspection indeed), its style felt clichéd and over-worn, its range of reference and allusion clearly limited to someone who had little knowledge or experience of the world, and its characterisation felt increasingly threadbare. Not dissuaded, however, Fouquet began (much in the manner of the aforementioned Nabokov) to amend. At first he simply embellished Yevachev's style a little here and there, figuring that since the original was so obscure no one would notice his additions (or improvements, as he thought of them). Then he began to extend the range of the work by

---

* But you, dear reader, can look at entry no. 50.

the addition of footnotes, including commentaries on what he supposed was the tale's genesis (he invented a long story about the titular widow, for example, supposing her to have been an early erotic obsession of Yevachev's). Each choice he made as a translator he rigorously annotated (giving rise to a lengthy disquisition on the frustrating, for a translator at least, lack of articles in the Russian language, as well as another fascinating essay on early Soviet-era Muscovite street slang).

Six years later, Fouquet had created a work which bore little of the source text, one which was not even a version or—as current fashionable parlance may have it—a 're-imagining' of 'The Widow's Legs,' but an entirely new work. He had, perhaps unfortunately, liberally interpreted the title too, coming up with 'An Older Single Woman's Lower Limbs.'

Finding no publisher for his work, he used the last of his inheritance to print up a number of copies himself. None were sold. (In a curious twist of fate, his father unknowingly rebought the entire print run, had them pulped and recycled into perfumed envelopes.)

J. D. 'JACK' FFRENCH

WHILE STRASBERG AND STANISLAVSKI'S 'method' is well known in the theatrical world, J. D. 'Jack' Ffrench was, perhaps, the first man who attempted to method *write*. Eschewing the timid road of second-hand research, Ffrench attempted to create veracity by fully living the stories he composed. His project was intriguing, but perhaps not one best undertaken by a man aiming to be a crime writer.

J. D. 'Jack' Ffrench first appeared in the late 1950s as crime reporter at the *North British Daily Advertiser*, where he worked on the notorious cases of the White Handbag Murders, the Chip Shop Killer and the Fake Butler Scandal before, ostensibly having been inspired by such intricate and macabre events, heading to London and deciding to write pure fiction. It was perhaps the failure of his first novel *Murderer's Wink* (a golden age–style caper involving handbags, chip shop proprietors and dubious household staff) which inspired him to start using the method. It was no longer enough to do the work other writers scrupulously undertake: Ffrench now had to inhabit his narratives entirely, and blur the boundaries between reportage and fiction.

Due to this, the following account of Ffrench's career is not based on the *BDLF*'s usual research sources but draws on the perhaps more reliable public archive of the Metropolitan Police.

In London in the sixties, Ffrench found his métier. He frequented Esmeralda's Barn, Murray's Cabaret and the Astor Club, meeting the Krays (one nark filed a report suggesting he may even have had an affair with Ronnie) and working as an estate agent for Peter Rachman. He shared cocktails with Christine Keeler and slept with Stewart Home's mother. He knew the forger Eric Quayne.* Not even having his hand nailed to a table by 'Mad' Frankie Fraser deterred his resolve.

As for many artists, the seventies seemed to disappear a little for Ffrench, but rumours that pieces of his body are still stored in the cellars of the Blind Beggar would seem to

* See entry no. 30.

be disproved by CIA files which note the presence of a certain 'French Jack' brokering deals between the New York and Sicilian mafias. The Italian poet and performance artist Fausto Squattrinato also claims to have met him during this time, but his evidence is always unreliable.

At this point, a novel still unforthcoming, it seems reasonable to speculate that Ffrench's criminal work had become more important to him than writing. The life of an international arms or drugs smuggler is almost certainly more remunerative than that of a writer, though somewhat more risk-bearing.

It is disappointing that an account of his work with the Cosa Nostra has never emerged, as the southern Italian organised crime organisations have always been flattered by the charms of fiction (though much less so by those of journalism: perhaps it is this that explains its absence, and even Ffrench's eventual demise).

His end was inevitable, though his body has never been found. Whether Ffrench is now holding up a turnpike in New Jersey, providing food for fish in some sludgy corner of the Mediterranean or waiting to be dredged from a murky London canal, we will never read the novel he wrote.

WELLON FREUND

IT IS KNOWN that writers are prone to addiction. For Sheridan LeFanu it was green tea, for Thomas De Quincey opium, and Balzac drank fifty cups of coffee a day (eventually poisoning himself with raw beans, so desperate was he for his hit). Elizabeth Barrett Browning favoured port and laudanum, while Kerouac typed his way to fame and obliteration on benzedrines. Modern commentators may claim Byron was a sex addict, while Dostoevsky himself acknowledged his addiction to the gaming tables (and how odd it would be to imagine him today, hanging around Betfred while not hooked up to Poker 888).

For Wellon Freund, not unusually for his generation, it was marijuana.

Fortunate to be born at the end of the Second World War, thus too old to get drafted to Vietnam, Freund still made it his business to protest as best he could, mostly by rolling carrot-size reefers on the covers of Quicksilver Messenger Service LPs.

So far, so typical. But what singled Freund out from his weed-addled comrades was that, as the clouds of the 1960s began to thin, Freund found himself possessed no longer to watch Cheech and Chong movies or to make midnight dashes for cookie dough ice cream, but to write.

Throughout the early 1970s, Freund would skin up and sit down at his IBM Selectric II to bash out tales of those who had tuned in, turned on and drifted off. His works could have made a major contribution to the literature of the period, but sadly most remained unfinished as the Selectric's ribbon often ran out, and by the time Freund had got hold of a replacement, he found he could no longer remember what it was he was writing. His only success of the period was composing the lyrics for a solo album by the bass player from Iron Butterfly (sadly, never released).

It was during this period that he claimed to have written the original screenplay for Perkins Cobb's great cult film *My Sweet Dread*, though Cobb himself denied this. ('Wellon Freund?' replied Cobb when asked about this. 'Who the hell is he?')

At the beginning of the 1980s, using the money he had made from his extra-literary activities, Freund invested in a five-hundred-acre farm in northern Utah, a place where he hoped to cultivate both of his passions. However, by now the tide had turned and one morning as Wellon sat behind his new Canon Typestar gazing out onto his crops, he saw a Federal plane swoop low and discharge several thousand litres of high-grade weed killer over his beloved plants.

At that point, Freund had been halfway through the opening sentence of what he believed would be his magnum opus, but finding himself unable to roll up and puff away, he was never able to complete so much as the first paragraph.

He spent a year trying to emulate Le Fanu by drinking gallons of green tea before breakfast, but found it had only diuretic rather than hallucinogenic effects. Then he tried Balzac's addiction, outdoing the father of realism by grinding beans and trying to snort them (which only ended up with him being hospitalised—not for a caffeine overdose, but for an imperfectly ground shard of Arabica which lodged itself in his upper nostril). He moved on to the various modish addictions of the age he found himself in: prescription meds (percosets merely made him fall asleep, Prozac unwilling to do anything at all), sex (an over-rated addiction, he decided, after contracting a particularly unpleasant STD), then moved back to the old standards, gambling and alcohol, but merely lost much of his fortune and poisoned his liver.

Nothing, it seemed, would ever bring his muse back.

Now Wellon Freund has cut his hair short, is a regis-

tered Republican and no longer believes Skip Spence's
Oar to be the masterpiece he once thought it. Incontinent,
broke and needing regular dialysis (when he can remember
his appointment time), he has not been near the Typestar for many years.

PASQUALE FRUNZIO

THE CITY OF TURIN is known for its chocolate, motorcars and literary suicides. Cesare Pavese overdosed on barbiturates in the Albergo Roma just opposite Porta Nuova railway station, while Primo Levi threw himself from the top of a stairwell in his apartment building on Corso Re Umberto. Swamped by debt and ripped off by his publisher, the swashbuckler Emilio Salgari used a barber's razor to perform an extravagant *seppuku* in the hills behind his house on Corso Casale. Friedrich Nietzsche took his time to die, but began the process by throwing his arms around a horse's neck and weeping extravagantly on Piazza Carlo Alberto, never again composing a legible word.

It is for this reason, perhaps, that Pasquale Frunzio moved to the city, taking up a dull job with the Italian state insurance company while working on *Lo Specchio Segreto*, a slim collection of late modernist verse. *Pace* Kafka, Pessoa and Svevo (all major influences), Frunzio was a quiet, modest man, who bided his time in the Inpdap offices unnoticed and spent his evenings working on his poems, no extravagance greater than a plate of *pasta asciutta* and a bottle of seltzer water.

While most writers will have considered the persistence of their reputation postmortem, few will have actively considered death as a career strategy. Not so Pasquale Frunzio. Frustrated by his inability to get any of his work into print, or even to get anyone to read it, he exercised the calculating logic and methodical precision praised by his day job, and decided to kill himself. Only then, Frunzio believed, would his work be noticed.

Frunzio carefully wrote a letter (one of his finest works, he thought, which would surely eventually form the preface to his *opera omnia*) and placed it on the table in the living room of his small flat in San Salvario, together with a clearly typed manuscript of *Lo Specchio Segreto*.

He then put on his best blue suit and (probably inspired by Sylvia Plath) turned on his gas oven, opened the door and placed his head in it. However, at the moment when the fumes were beginning to take effect, his doorbell rang. Though Frunzio was somewhat drowsy at this point, he was always a man of regular, polite habit, and dragged himself off the kitchen floor to answer. A postman stood at the door bearing a telegram from none other than the esteemed publisher Giangiacomo Feltrinelli, expressing apologies for the accidental return of *Lo Specchio Segreto*, which he considered a masterpiece and wished to publish post haste. Taken aback by this unexpected reversal, Frunzio sat down at his desk and, wanting to read the telegram more carefully to make sure he hadn't misunderstood it, turned on the light. A spark from the switch ignited the cloud of gas which had, by now, filled his apartment, resulting in a large explosion and completely immolating Frunzio, his farewell letter and all of his work of which— in a rare lapse—he had made no copy.

'THE GOATHERD POET'

ANTIQUITY'S A BUGGER. Not only did you have to live a thousand or so years before anyone had even thought of the printing press but if you wanted to avoid the slippery oral tradition you would have had to scratch your work into rock or daub dubious ink onto an animal skin. Then you'd have to put up with centuries of fire, flood, famine, pestilence and war doing their usual tricks, as well as the possibly even greater threat of the vagaries of literary fashion. Sadly, an ancient poet looking to insert him- or herself into eternity was probably knackered before he, or she, even started. We have no idea how many great works have been lost, yet we are aware of a number of bafflingly mediocre

ones which have managed to survive and even get canon-
ised. (Have you ever read *Beowulf*?)

Pity, then, if you will, a poor man known only as the
Goatherd Poet. No name other than this recalls him, he
may have not even been a man, he may have been a group
of people. The only thing we know for certain about the
Goatherd Poet is that sometime between the beginning of
the eighth and the end of the eleventh centuries he wrote a
poem called *The Goatherd*.

We would like to imagine the Goatherd Poet as a rough
man of the earth, a proto-Romantic outsider, an early psy-
chogeographer tracing his way across the northern part
of his nation, faithful herd at his heel, grappling with the
metre of this rough language. Historians, however, doubt
this possibility, and it is probably more likely the poet was
the second or third son of a Saxon chieftain, less given to
the pleasures of the meadhall or the broadsword, trying to
make himself useful or get a foothold sideways across the
social scale into the Bardic class.

The poem, sources tell us, was an alliterative epic, some
thousand lines long, recording the life of a lonely goatswain
as he wanders a bleak landscape, lamenting the obscure
loss of his homeland and the bitterness of *wyrd* fate. It was
held by one of the few people who claim to have seen a
copy to have been a greater work than *The Wanderer*, more
challenging than *The Seafarer*, wider in scope and richer in
literary and imaginative resource than *Pearl*.

A single copy of the poem—allegedly written in the poet's

own hand rather than having been botchedly transcribed by some short-sighted or easily distracted monk—survived in an island abbey off the coast of Northumbria, where it lay undisturbed for centuries, miraculously surviving the sacking of the monasteries and a rampant fire in the late fifteenth century. When the abbey eventually collapsed into the sea in 1760, the mouldering remains of its library were broken up and dispersed across Europe, where they fell into the hands of collectors and antiquarians. After some travels, *The Goatherd* ended up in the library of a vast country estate in Hampshire, owned by the great-grandfather of Sir Belmont Rossiter.* It was not placed on the library's shelves, however, but used as material to shore up the walls of the crumbling building, and there it sat, holding up the wainscoting until Sir Belmont had the place rebuilt. On the discovery of this ancient, rotting sheaf, Rossiter became an early champion of the poem. He went on to write an entire history of Goatherd verse, though his nimbler Victorian peers accused him of having invented not only the poem but also the poet, and indeed the entire genre.

When Rossiter fell into obscurity, so did his work and those authors he had championed. The house collapsed and was used as a hospital during the First World War. It is believed the inmates used the ancient manuscript as paper with which to roll cigarettes. We earnestly hope the great work bought its smokers some pleasure.

---

* See entry no. 34.

VIRGIL HAACK

THOUGH INITIALLY HELD in disregard by more conservative critics, minimalism has now become an entirely respectable genre in the fields of music and the visual arts. It seems a shame, therefore, that it has never received its due laurels in the literary arena.

While the works of writers ranging from Samuel Beckett to Raymond Carver to Donald Barthelme and Lydia Davis have variously been described as having something minimalist about them, and while haiku and flash fiction are widely practised forms, few writers have ever really dared to grasp the baton held out by Morton Feldman or Steve Reich, to face the challenge laid down by Donald

Judd or Barnett Newman, or to follow the map drawn up by Mies van der Rohe or Kazimir Malevich's Suprematists.

One of these brave few was Virgil Haack.

Haack (described by those who knew him as having a prominent nose set into a long ovoid face between two tiny eyes, as though his own head were already a minimalist work) first appeared in New York in what may have been minimalism's *annus mirabilis*, 1964, carrying nothing but a small bag containing a Hermes Rocket (that most minimal of instruments), flitting from white-walled galleries to bleak loft spaces, apocryphally taking part in the debut performance of *In C* while frantically trying to edit his five-hundred-page beat-influenced novel down to something which more closely matched the tenor of the times.

After several years' work, Haack (perhaps unsurprisingly described by those who knew him as 'a man of few words') had managed to finish his endeavour and duly sent out the manuscript of *Untitled Work (No. 1)* to agents and publishers throughout the city. Convinced that less was certainly more, he had written the single word 'I' on the first, and only, page of his novel.

Unfortunately (perhaps due to the inadequacies of the Hermes Rocket), the agents and editors of New York unanimously mistook that lonely, passionate word for the number 'one' and believed that Haack had forgotten to enclose the ensuing chapters of his great work.

Undeterred, Haack moved into a room in a building occupied by La Monte Young (an admirer of his work) and thus became exposed to the idea of the eternal minimal. (Long drones fed through the house in permanent, gently fluctuating G, C, C# and D chord progressions.) Here he took part in his only known public reading: Angus MacLise battered a dustbin lid and Tony Conrad scraped his violin while Haack intoned a single phoneme. The performance went on for three days, after which Haack collapsed in exhaustion.

By now obsessed with duration, Haack picked himself up and began work on his next book, a work which consisted of the same word typed over and over and over again. Forty-five years and several hundred typewriter ribbons later, Haack is still typing, and no one knows what that single word is.

CHARLES HÉBÉ

LATE ONE WINTER NIGHT in 1904, sitting in his well-appointed study in a spacious apartment just off the Avenue Fouquet, drinking kir (as well as, he would later admit, a little absinthe) and smoking a good pipe, having been inspired by the wild conversation of his friends over a dinner of paddlefish roe, black olive tapenade and aubergine bottarga on crisp pumpernickel, Charles Hébé, previously untouched by literary pretensions, took up his pen and began to write.

In later years, as he dragged himself from park bench to shoddy boardinghouse in a sequence of ever-drearier towns, Hébé would remember that night as the only moment of greatness in his life, and regret it bitterly.

Inspired by the whirling talk of his artistic companions and the fervid atmosphere of the city in that period,

Hébé had engendered the stuff of literary legend. Out of fauvism, early surrealism, alcohol and opium-induced reveries, nascent psychoanalysis and too much reading of Baudelaire, Laforgue, Nerval and various other symbolists and imagists, Hébé had written the first draft of a novel centred on the monstrous character of *Oncle Cauchemère* (the only attempted English translation of the work rendered the character's name as 'Uncle Sandwoman'), a great swaggering brute of a person, by turns hilarious and terrifying, as real and as intangible as a nightmare.

He showed the manuscript to his friends, who all acclaimed it wildly, writing deranged songs celebrating the adventures of Oncle Cauchemère, trying to stage a play based on the story (though no actor was found who could take on such a challenging role), and drawing or painting visionary, oneiric pictures of the handsome hulking psychopath, charming women and eating children. Only one of these portraits still exists, sadly, now housed in the storage room of a provincial museum in Alsace.

Oncle Cauchemère is a unique figure in literary history: although he draws on mythical and fairytale archetype, there is something distinctly and uncannily real about him. (Hébé himself, in a rare comment, claimed the figure was based on a distant relative he half-remembered from his childhood.) He is imbued with a human heft that owes everything to great nineteenth-century French realism. This, according to sources, was what was most terrifying about Cauchemère: he was entirely believable.

All too believable for Hébé, it seemed. While word of

his great work spread throughout the city, no publisher was prepared to touch Hébé's manuscript, and the character rapidly became the stuff of legend. Hébé began to receive mail addressed to 'Oncle Cauchemère,' and had to turn down frequent requests from journalists wishing to interview the man. Despite being a wiry, spindly little man himself, his acquaintances began to nickname Hébé with the name of his creation.

One night, following an attempt by a gang of drunken aesthetes to break into his apartment demanding to meet Oncle Cauchemère, Hébé sat down for a second time and tried to write: at the top of the page he put down the words *La mort d'Oncle Cauchemère*. Having invented such a terrible character, he realised, he now had to kill him.

His attempts, it seems, were not successful.

Little else was heard from Charles Hébé after that night: his friends received occasional postcards or increasingly deranged letters from small northern towns, Lens, Le Havre, Fécamp, some asserting that Cauchemère, or someone impersonating him, was trying to kill his own author. Legal deeds recount that Hébé sold his elegant apartment but nevertheless fell into poverty, drinking ever more and always trying to finish his second great work, one that would set him free of the first.

In December 1911, police in Caen had to break into a room in the Pension Jarry, where Hébé had last been seen. The room was empty, save for the torn remnants of a manuscript. The police report mentions teeth marks, as though it had been attemptedly eaten.

HANS KAFKA

'NOMINATIVE DETERMINISM' is a slippery idea, and one that may not withstand the fierce glare of sustained critical scrutiny. Yet perhaps there is something about the name 'Kafka' (which, somewhat disappointingly, means only 'jackdaw' in Czech) that may lead its bearer into dangerous graphomaniac tendencies. Here, we refer not to the famous angst-ridden Germanic writer but to his lesser-known near-cognate, Hans Kafka.

Tracing through the records as far as we can, we find no family connection between the two authors, though 'Kafka' is a far from common name. Is this mere coincidence, a unique combination of time, place and circumstance or something about the thieving *corvus monedula* which drives its namesakes into the thankless business of writing?

Hans Kafka was born in 1883 just across the street from the other Kafka family, son to a seamstress and a successful retailer of fancy goods. As a child, he heard of his neighbouring namesakes but was told by his domineering father to have nothing to do with them.

A quiet, diligent boy, he left school and enrolled in the law faculty at Charles University, but then changed to pursue the study of chemistry (narrowly missing that other writer, who made the same journey in the opposite direction), and on graduating took on work as an analytical chemist, a job he would keep for the rest of his life. He helped to develop an early form of asbestos and used his scarce free time to write a number of challenging short stories.

He sent these early stories to the journals *Hyperion* and *Arkadia* but was turned down with a series of baffling rejection letters. *Dear Sir*, they began. *We are endeavouring to publish your work. Please do not feel the necessity to send us more pieces under a clumsy pseudonym.*

As yet unaware of the fate of his almost homonymous former neighbour, Kafka did not let the rejections dissuade him and began work on his first full-length piece, a grotesque tale of a beetle who is transformed into a man.

You know how this story will go on: manuscripts lost, burned or denied, failed love affairs, the sustained support of a tiny handful of close friends, the inevitable onset of a lingering, rotting disease. Kafka did not disappoint. However, a crucial difference lay in the fact that the illness from which Kafka suffered throughout his twenties and thirties turned out not to be tuberculosis after all, but nothing more than a nasty cold which, due to his poor diet, damp flat and the inclement weather conditions of the Czech capital, he did not manage to shake off for several years.

Unlike his near-namesake, Hans Kafka lived and even managed to survive the brutality of the 1940s. By force of sheer miracle, he slipped slowly and quietly into postwar Czech life, his singed manuscripts still packed in a suitcase under the bed of his small apartment on the Sokolovská, watching the reputation of the boy from across the street who almost had the same name as him grow and grow.

As an old man, as he went out to get his morning *becherovka*, he saw tourists wandering the streets of his city wearing T-shirts bearing a picture of the dark-eyed, skinny-faced boy he remembered. He put his hand on the cool glass and rolled a cigarette. I'm alive, he thought as he sipped the bitter liqueur and drew on the warm smoke. I am alive.

YILDIRIM KEMAL

YILDIRIM KEMAL WORKS in a kebab shop on the Kingsland Road in Dalston. As he slices doner meat, skewers shish kebabs and adds chilli sauce to the takeaway requirements of the glazed or belligerent drunks of his late-night clientele, he takes a strange pride in the fact that none of them know he is a poet.

The young Kemal won the Greater Istanbul Under 18s Poetry competition for a late-Ottoman-style elegy on the death of a gazelle. Though they thought it derivative, the judges nonetheless awarded it first prize, taking the work to be a clever allegory on contemporary Turkish politics (though, in reality, it was inspired by a wildlife documentary Kemal had seen on television).

Kemal's mother was proud to have a poet in the family, and encouraged her son to write more. Having drawn as far as he could on the natural world, Kemal changed his focus to urban life, and his style to that of Nazim Hikmet rather than his illustrious predecessors of the Sublime Porte. His mother was not impressed, so Kemal downed his pen, left school and went to work in his uncle's import-export business. The brief sip of success and the call of the muse were too strong, however, and Kemal spent most of his days working on hard-edged modernist verse rather than on the bills of lading which piled up before him. In a bid to prove to his despairing sister that her son was not useless, and to rid himself of an unproductive employee, Kemal's uncle forwarded a (not insubstantial) sum of money to a small publisher, who, in turn, produced a run of 2,500 copies of a slim volume of this talented young poet's verse.

It sold one copy.

Kemal's mother didn't even buy one, hoping she would get a free book from her son or her brother (who had neglected to mention the question of author copies in the hastily written contract for the deal), neither of whom obliged. Kemal was crushed by this lack of success and, deciding his problem was the limited audience for Turkish-language poetry, decided to move to the UK to improve his English.

One could ask why Yildirim Kemal has been included at all in the *BDLF*. One sale of a published book is, after all, far greater success than many other entries have achieved.

Moby-Dick sold but a handful of copies on its first appearance, and *Wuthering Heights* even fewer.

The sad fact is that the one person who purchased Kemal's collection did so believing it to be a book of verse penned by the eponymous Hacettepe S.K. centre forward. On discovering his mistake, the purchaser, an Ankaran octogenarian, unbound the book and each day used one of Kemal's poems to wrap his lunchtime kebab.

Yet this matters not. Each night, as Kemal stuffs salad into pita and drizzles garlic sauce on grilled chicken, he thinks of the one person out there in Diyarbakir or Batman, in Erzurum or Van, in Fener or Cihangir reading his work, and dreaming.

JÜRGEN KITTLER

⌁WHILE THE CONNECTIONS between literature and political activism have been widely examined, those between literature and terrorism are less well known. The Russian anarchist-poets of the Mauve February movement claimed to have thrown ink-pots along with their hand-made bombs in the 1890s, but have left little trace in official histories of revolution or literature. The so-called *manos pintadas* may have formed an armed vanguard group in the 1910 Mexican revolution, but remain so obscure that not even Roberto Bolaño has ever mentioned them. The Italian poet and performance artist Fausto Squattrinato claimed to have taken part in the kidnapping of Aldo Moro in 1978, but he is a known liar.

Truth be told, most poets have felt happier composing sonnets about revolutions rather than ever actually dirtying their hands with them.

It is precisely this which makes the case of Jürgen Kittler so much more fascinating. Little is certain about this shady figure who flitted through Europe, North Africa and the Middle East under a series of bizarre aliases between the years of 1957 and 1989 (in which year his series of incendiary typewritten communiqués dried up), and there are those, indeed, who go so far as to claim that Jürgen Kittler was only ever an alias for yet another even shadowier figure.

Kittler first appeared hanging around the fringes of the Letterist International (themselves already a fringe group) before denouncing them as bourgeois collaborationists in his 1957 pamphlet *Le monde n'est pas sur le feu. Encore* (variously translated as 'The world is not on fire. Yet' and 'The world is not on fire. Again'), and reappeared in the early sixties in locations as diverse as Tangiers, New York, Geneva, London, Cap d'Antibes, Düsseldorf and Manchester (at least according to the postmarks of the various letters, poems, diatribes, novels and outright threats he sent to a number of international publications during this period). He was almost certainly photographed alongside Daniel Cohn-Bendit and Jean-Paul Sartre during *les événements* (and has even been credited with authoring a number of the most dazzling slogans of that golden age of the slogan).

His mature period commenced shortly after this, when in retreat from what he saw as the grave disappointment, not to say betrayal, of '68, he wrote what some claim to be his greatest work, a manifesto issued from a hideout somewhere in the Pyrenees. *Towards a Revolution of the Word* exists, confusingly, in a number of different versions, some called *Towards a Revolution of the World*. It is uncertain if Kittler meant to play on this close homograph or if the 'l' key on his typewriter, a portable Olympia Splendid 66, was merely defective. Whatever, the work insisted that revolution could be brought about not through a total rebuilding of the social order, but only through the rebuilding of language itself.

His attempts to rebuild language itself resulted in most of his 1970s works, which even according to his most fervent disciples are largely incomprehensible.

Despite this, the '70s may well have been his most active period, in which Kittler reappears (as Georges Sansou, Jürgen Mittelos and, confusingly, as Eric Quayne), playing bass for the Krautrock group Lustfaust and Mancunian post-punk outfit King Ink, frequenting the Red Army Faction in Düsseldorf, the *Brigate Rosse* in Rome and the Angry Brigade in London, stealing cars with Jean Genet in Marseille, playing golf with Carlos the Jackal in Lebanon and posing for a rare Gerhard Richter portrait in Berlin, while all the time circulating samizdat versions of his work.

None of these were ever published, allegedly due to their devastating revolutionary potential, though this is a difficult claim to justify as anyone who has read any of Kittler's work from this period is now dead, in a maximum-security prison or has vanished. It has been claimed that copies of his work are being held in government archives in the UK, France, Germany, Italy and the United States, but all are subject to a hundred-year embargo, and will not be read by any of us currently living.

MARTA KUPKA

FEW OF US ever get what we really want for Christmas. While the most fortunate amongst us may unwrap an old-time Parcheesi board, a book we'd never heard of but which looks fascinating or even a humble dozen home-baked cookies, no one ever gets a guaranteed readership, lifelong respect or happiness. No parcel, no matter how beautifully wrapped in a big red box with a gold ribbon tied around it, will bring your lover back.

On Christmas Day in 1948, Marta Kupka, having been a bookish child, much given to scribbling stories in thin paper notebooks, was awarded a Royal Quiet Deluxe by her parents, who had found a contact, scraped together enough money and, anxious to encourage their only daughter's nascent literary talent, managed to acquire the piece of precision American engineering.

The machine was wrapped in thick brown parcel paper, and so it stayed for the next sixty-four years.

For Kupka, brought up on powdered eggs and bread filled out with sawdust, the gift (whose nature she had guessed, being an intelligent child) represented an unimaginable luxury. Once unwrapped, she knew it would sit on her small desk, gleaming, filled with promise, and yet also with threat.

Over the next few years she occasionally imagined rolling a sheet of paper into it, and dutifully typing out sentences from a Pitman course about quick brown foxes and lazy dogs, training her fingers to follow the keys which would reproduce the stories in her mind.

The sheer weight of the thing, not only physically, but also metaphorically, bore down on her so much that she could not bear to sully its keys with a tale she considered less than perfect. Much as some second-novelists are said to be paralysed in the face of following up a successful debut, Kupka could not even find the perfect first word to begin to glean her teeming brain. And so the gift remained unopened.

But when she was eighty, on Christmas Day, she uncovered the Royal Quiet Deluxe, long hidden under the piles of letters, postcards and legal documents which had made up her life since then, and finally removed the thick brown paper, keeping the now-faded tag (*'from mammi and papi, with our best wishes'*), and was delighted to find the keys, though creaky, still functioning.

She quickly dusted the typewriter off, sat down, and began to write.

Sadly, although the intervening years had been kind to the typewriter, they had taken their toll on Kupka's eyesight, and she failed to notice that the once well-inked ribbon had now dried up completely. She wrote incessantly for three weeks, completing the long tale of her life, failing to see that not a single word of what she wrote actually made it onto the paper.

ELISE LA RUE

THE ENIGMATIC AUTHORESS Elise La Rue (and while we generally applaud the move to gender-neutral appellations, La Rue was quite definitely an *authoress*) first appeared in the 1890s as a soubrette on the (by now far past its best) Paris stage, taking the lead in a series of long-forgotten revues with titles such as *L'amour est comment il est perdu, pas comment il a trouvé*. Toulouse-Lautrec lamented his inability to paint her: 'She wasn't born, she was created,' he allegedly remarked of her, a comment which may have been true—there is no trace of her birthplace, nationality, parentage or ancestry anywhere. The enigmatic La Rue (she later tried to have the epithet added to her birth certificate, although unfortunately no birth certificate ever existed for her, so this wish proved impossible) variously claimed to be French, German, Polish, Russian and American at various stages in her life. This shifting quality, along with her effect upon men, made her prime material to be a spy during the First World War, a role which she took on with gusto, working in espionage for no less than six of the engaged nations, mostly at the same time.

Following this period there are a few lost years in which she seems to have adopted a number of aliases: turning up in the nascent Hollywood as an aspiring starlet variously trying the soubriquets of Theodesia Purr, Vera Palmer and Katie Hedmore; trying her hand at writing Latin-flavoured erotica under the name of Juana Edelmira; holding séances as Margaretha Zella-St. Cyr; and penning an agony aunt column as Phyllis Delphia.

It was a few years after the conflict that she discovered her muse, and on returning to Europe recalled the favours owing to her by a number of European nations by occupying elegant flats in Mayfair, Manhattan, Trastevere and the third arrondissement, where she instituted a number of literary salons. Most of the great writers of the age paid her court, though few sadly recorded the occasion. It is said that Zelda Fitzgerald and Hadley Hemingway both tried to have her poisoned while Nora Joyce called her a 'trollop' (though this didn't stop her being one of the many suggested models for Molly Bloom).

She wrote longhand, naked, voluptuously, lying on her

divan, usually covered in the fur of a snow leopard which she claimed she had herself skinned from the back of the animal (this story, improbable as it may seem, may be true: records that have recently come to light show she assisted the young Stalin on a hunting trip through the central Asian wilds), accompanied by her favourite cocktail of schnapps and Dubonnet (which she called a 'Bloody Murder'), beginning mid-morning and knocking off shortly before lunch.

Having started and abandoned several novels, she always claimed her greatest work was her play 'The Heart Is an Autumn Wanderer,' a loosely biographical five-hour epic requiring a cast of some two hundred people. The fact that it was never performed she put down to mysterious conspiracies at work in the theatrical cultures of London, Paris, New York and Berlin. (She ignored the fact that her second play, 'Nakedness Tonight,' which featured only two performers and one role, was similarly rejected.)

Her profligacy was legendary: in his dazzling memoir *The Girl with the Avant-Garde Face*, Eric Levallois recalls how, having run out of paper, she wrote Imagist poems on five hundred franc notes.

In later years, she befriended Anaïs Nin and Henry Miller, and is fondly recalled in some of their diaries and correspondence (Nin called her 'The Duchess', Miller 'a stinking rotting whore'). She wrote long, rambling letters, making copies of each one for herself and for posterity, in perfumed ink, on violet notepaper.

Following the Second World War, her fortunes changed dramatically. Henry Miller, the Hemingways and the Joyces having long since passed on, she felt the golden age of literary Paris had passed. Nin removed all mention of La Rue from the published version of her diaries. Sartre failed to recognise her. She fell into black depressions, her alcohol consumption rose dramatically. Ever short of money, she tried to call in favours but her once-ardent admirers had now either vanished or claimed to have no memory of this stinking, shrivelled woman. By 1961, she was living on the street, sleeping under the Pont Neuf, her letters, their violet perfume now long departed, keeping her warm through the cold nights. In 1967, she was knifed to death by a fellow vagrant who mistook the sheaves of paper for bank notes.

MAXWELL LOEB

IF YOU EVER LOOK at a picture of the Beats, among the poets, junkies and general hangers-on, somewhere behind Ginsberg's beard or Burroughs's hat, leaning over Kerouac's shoulder or looking thoughtfully at Neal Cassady, you will always see one person unlabelled and upon whose identity critics and historians never quite agree. That person is almost certainly Maxwell Loeb.

Maxwell (who insisted on pronouncing his surname *loob*, which may not have helped his chances in life) was born in 1928 in an airy Upper West Side apartment block, the son of a couple of psychoanalysts (one Freudian, one Jungian). Having schooled unremarkably, in 1942 he attempted to enlist, only to be laughed out of the building by the recruiting sergeant, an experience which bruised him into becoming a lifelong adherent of the counter-culture, a questioner of authority, a hipster, a hippie.

Being in New York and in his twenties during the 1950s, Maxwell Loeb was blessed, golden. He action-painted, be-bopped and free-jazzed. He popped bennies, chewed pey-ote, sank whisky sours and sang hootenanny folk. He gave Jack Kerouac lifts in his parents' Buick Riviera, stood on the Brooklyn Bridge and modelled for Nat Tate, ran green whenever Herbert Huncke showed up and trav-elled to Tangiers where he danced in his tighty-whiteys for Allen Ginsberg. He saw the best minds of his gener-ation slumped asleep on toilets and began to believe his first thought his best thought.

Unfortunately, Maxwell's first thoughts were usually of hamantaschen, chopped herring salad and the inner elbows of young women (a curious fixation which his par-ents would have no doubt found fascinating). In the hands of William Carlos Williams or Gary Snyder, this may have been promising material, but Maxwell turned out to have little aptitude for verse (Ginsberg's dismissal of 'yellow morning stanzas of gibberish' in *Howl* is probably refer-encing Loeb's *In the Scarlet Bathtub*).

Despite his mentor's opprobrium, Maxwell continued to write, frequently and copiously, and soon discovered that though his literary talents were not admired, the sheer speed of his typing was. This was no small gift in the feverish environment of the Beats, and soon Maxwell found himself the centre of a small cult dedicated to the worship of the Remington No. 5 and the Hermes 3000. Loeb's ability to manipulate such machines at speeds of more than 130 words per minute earned him envy and praise in equal measures.

Maxwell became a master of technique, and bothered little about content or style. He felt Truman Capote's epithet 'That's not writing, that's typing' directed at himself rather than at *On the Road* and took it as a compliment. Long after his comrades had died, moved back in with their mothers, vanished in Kathmandu or moved upstate and got respectable, Loeb continued to type, only the increasing difficulty of finding typewriter ribbons slowing him. One day, we fear, they will cease to exist altogether and only then will Maxwell Loeb finally complete his life's work.

MAXIM MAKSIMICH

ONE APRIL MORNING in 1862, Maxim Maksimich set off early so as not to miss the first steamer of the season, the one that would take him up the rapidly thawing river as far as Tomsk, then Perm, then Chelyabinsk or Ufa, across Siberia and through the Urals to Yekaterinburg and the eventual west. There, he believed, he would board a train for Moscow, where he would find some work teaching, a small room in a boardinghouse and then, in time, a wife, and then, in time, having published a chain of stories in respected literary gazettes, fame.

It didn't happen that way.

After three weeks on board, during which time his ship

had made only a tortuous few miles along the unexpect-edly ice-bound river, Maksimich tired of the endless diet of kasha, salt fish and Georgian brandy. When the *Princess of the Rhine* (in later years Maksimich would often wonder how the single-funnelled ship had ended up so far from home) stopped to refuel at an apparently nameless town, he went ashore and found himself in a small hos-telry, drank several flagons of the local kvass and woke up in a haystack two days later. He discovered he had been robbed of everything he owned, including the laboriously handwritten manuscript of *The Christ of the Cornfields*. He ran to the boarding platform only to find the *Princess* had left some hours before.

At first, other than ruing the loss of what he believed was his masterpiece, Maksimich worried little, figuring that another steamer would be along soon. He didn't realise that the *Princess of the Rhine* (due to its inebriated Bavar-ian captain) had lost itself hopelessly along a neglected tributary, one no other steamship passed along for that entire year, nor the next, nor the one after that. He tried not to worry and told himself the railway would soon ar-rive in the small town (which he eventually found did have a name at least, though little more), and that surely within a year or two he would be reaping the benefits of his la-bours, ensconced in a comfortable Muscovite townhouse, gazing adoringly at his devoted wife, who would sit pa-tiently copying out his manuscripts for him while he en-gaged in a rubber of bridge with Lev or Anton or Fyodor.

He spent the next fifty years in the town, waiting for the locomotives to arrive or a ship to depart, occasionally contemplating taking a carriage through the thick forest, but always thinking better of the idea, slowly composing a series of stories commemorating village life as the turn of the century approached then passed, largely unnoticed.

He died in 1912, impaled by a falling icicle, a casualty of the thaw for which he had waited so long.

In 1992, on the eightieth anniversary of his death, some local townsfolk who valued their literary heritage set up a museum in Maxim Maksimich's honour. His living room and study are preserved exactly as they would have been during his heyday: a quill pen lies on the rough wooden desk alongside a quire of paper, an embroidered blanket is thrown across a sagging sofa, a samovar is filled with water ready to be boiled to prepare the linden tea he adored so much. The museum has limited visiting hours, however, and during the thirty years it has been open, not a single visitor has passed through its doors.

EDWARD NASH

WHEN EDWARD NASH was found dead at the age of forty-eight, sitting on the bench at the top of the cliff which overlooked the sea in the small town where he lived, few were surprised.

A known character in the town, Nash spoke to few but was always to be seen sitting on that bench, apparently doing nothing other than staring at the sea and the sky.

For many years, a small inheritance and a frugal lifestyle having given him freedom from a deadening job, he had gone each and every day to that same point on the hillside, sometimes at dawn, sometimes at dusk and sometimes from one to the other, and sat there, and looked out.

Stories were muttered in the town: he was waiting for a ship to come in, he was a spy, a smuggler or a drug-trafficker, a birdwatcher, perhaps an idle eccentric or a man confronting mental health issues in his own unique way. None of these stories were true.

After closely observing the sea and the clouds for at least six hours each day, Edward Nash would return home and begin to write. His aim, both minute and monumental, was to describe as closely and as perfectly as possible the slow swell of a wave, from the moment it began to form to the point at which it foamed, crested and then broke on the shore or back on itself into the moiling water which was its source. His aim, both vast and insignificant, was to delineate the nature of a cloud, to use words to pinpoint its evanescence and eternity.

He firmly believed that one perfect sentence drawn from these two essential elements would capture everything that needed to be written: the touch of a lover's lips, the memory of a child's laughter or a close friend's death, the nature and significance of our place in this turbulent, beautiful, destructive, miraculous world. Everything that needed to be written, read and remembered, he thought, could be captured if only he could find the precise words to describe that wave, or that cloud.

It may be true that Nash was given to some kind of monomania, but what form of writing is not such?

On emptying the caravan where Nash had lived, the social workers consigned to deal with this friendless, unfamilied man's effects found a huge cache of notebooks stacked from floor to ceiling, lining the small space in which he had lived. Each notebook was full, but filled with only single words, lines or phrases. Like a wave or a cloud, Edward Nash's sentence never completed itself.

The bench remains there to this day, though few people sit there now, finding the spot too windy.

OTHA ORKKUT

$\curlyvee$OTHA ORKKUT (1890–1943) was a poet, translator and historian. She wrote two slim volumes of lyric verse (mostly celebrating the natural beauty of her homeland), and at the time of her death was composing a significantly longer work in the national-epic mode. She also wrote a history of her country, but as we shall see, this was but a short book. This meagre output would perhaps be unremarkable, as would Orkkut herself, were it not for the fact that she was the last surviving speaker of Cimbrian, which was the language in which all her works were composed. Indeed, Otha Orkkut's oeuvre is the only body of literature in that now sadly deceased language.

Language death is a disturbingly common phenomenon. Of the seven thousand or so languages currently spoken, only 10 percent will survive by the end of the next century, according to more pessimistic observers. Lipan, Totoro and Bikya are all currently down to a handful of speakers and not expected to see out the next decade. Many factors are at the root of this: the cultural hegemony of English, the expansion of Spanish or Chinese, imperialism, globalisation, the threatened habitats and changing life patterns of indigenous peoples across the world. A museum is needed to preserve what is passing away largely unnoticed.

If such a museum were to be built, we hope that Otha Orkkut would take her place, representing the great Cimbrian tongue. Cimbrian was a Bothno-Ugaric language, the language of a group of people from the northeasternmost corner of Europe, an unhappy people who only managed to establish their own state very briefly: Orkkut's father declared the existence of the People's Republic of Cimbria at midday on September 5th, 1918, only to have the armies of two of the country's more belligerent neighbours invade by teatime on that same day. (A strong spirit of Cimbrian nationalism survived, however, with a few Cimbrians refusing to recognise the legitimacy of the invaders and continuing to hold their own democratic parliament in the basement of Orkkut's parents' house.)

Orkkut was raised as the last monoglot Cimbrian and wrote verse from an early age. She lived all her life in a small house in Orkko on the Gulf of Bothnia, and never married.

Cimbrian, it is said, was a unique language in that it contained a tense which was used to describe a person or object which had gone missing or been lost: neither present nor past, still existing in a space or time which no non-Cimbrian can ever properly comprehend.

A number of critics and translators are currently at work on Orkkut's books, her manuscripts now inhabiting the realm of that unique Cimbrian tense. It is possible they will not be entirely lost to posterity. But what will be understood of them now that there is no one to recognise the exact feeling evoked by the words *kuttsruch* or *beja-manesch*? What nuance will be lost? Who can know precisely what Orkkut felt that last morning when the soldiers came to put her on a train and she packed her small bag, never to return? Who can translate that elusive verb form, existing and not-existing, neither here nor there?

KARL PILCROW

CONVINCED THAT THE APOCALYPSE was coming, Karl Pilcrow built himself an ark.

His ark, unlike that of Biblical renown, was largely constructed from old pieces of two-by-four, a disused chicken coop and an old sofa he'd found in the alley behind his home.

Pilcrow's ark, again unlike Noah's, was not meant to house generations of animals with which to repopulate the earth, but would contain a single thing: *The Book of Pilcrow*, a long series of aphorisms, insights and great truths he felt he had amassed during his life as a quantity surveyor, and which would give moral and spiritual guidance to the few people he believed would survive the end of the world as we know it.

The neighbours complained about the unsightly construction growing in their midst, which, somewhat surprisingly given the methods and materials of its construction, soon rose to a great height.

Council officials were called, and commanded Pilcrow to remove the ark. He refused, but fearing its destruction he decide to launch it onto the ship canal that ran behind his home.

The day of the launch was a watery one, mid-December, England, the rain falling and staying in the air as it only can there. The ark and its precious typewritten cargo were waterlogged before Pilcrow had even managed to use his Ford Fiesta to drag the thing into the murky green water.

It sank immediately, of course, and as the weather grew worse and worse, and strange portents appeared in the skies, Karl Pilcrow followed it into the water.

JOÃO QUARESMA

THOUGH JOYCE LEANS on his stick and peers down
North Earl Street, Pushkin presides over the endless traffic jam on Ulitsa Tverskaya and Dante scowls lugubriously
over almost every town square in Italy, statues of writers
are few. This may not be a bad thing: pity the land that
needs its heroes, warns Brecht's Galileo, and by extraction
pity the land that needs its statues. But dead writers? Are
they such a threat?

Whatever the theoretical complexities of such modes of
memorialisation, we would like to celebrate the statue of
João Quaresma, which stands in the central square of a
small town in northern Portugal.

Heavily influenced by fellow Lusitanian Camões, João Quaresma spent most of his life composing a single epic poem recording the exploits of the hardy *bacalhau* fishermen of the northern Atlantic. However, as the pages filled (eventually numbering over a thousand) and Quaresma grew older, the sensation that few, if any, would ever read his work became more and more real to him and he began to worry about his stake in immortality. Seeing as his day job was as a monumental mason (some of his finest lines are inscribed on various headstones scattered across the Alto Douro), in his spare time Quaresma set to carving his own statue, sure in the knowledge that after his demise his work would be recognised and his marble self-portrait would be ceremonially placed in one of the great squares of Lisbon or Porto.

Sadly, upon his death it emerged that Quaresma hadn't paid a single *escudo* of tax in his entire working life, and the impoverished local government came down hard on his widow, who had hoped to pay off her late husband's debts through the sale of his literary endeavours. The authorities, however, were more interested in the large amount of valuable Carrara marble that comprised Quaresma's self-portrait.

At that point in history, the Republican fervour sweeping the country resulted in the assassination of King Carlos I, and the mayor felt it would be a grand patriotic gesture to have a statue of his successor Manuel II erected in the centre of their small town. In this pre-visual age, few had much idea what the king looked like, so Quaresma's glasses were filed away and an impressive stucco moustache added to his face, and the statue was duly unveiled in October 1910, only days before Manuel ('the Unfortunate') fled into exile in England. Seeing as the figure pointed boldly toward the distant sea, it was hastily decided that it instead represented Vasco da Gama or Henry the Navigator. Few cared.

The moustache has fallen off now, but the statue still stands, smeared with graffiti debating the relative merits of Sporting Lisbon and FC Porto. Alongside Pessoa and his beloved Camões in Lisbon, João Quaresma is one of the few literary statues in Portugal, though today not only does no one know his work, no one knows it is him.

AURELIO QUATTROCHI

IN A LARGE ROOM on the fourth floor of an eighteenth-century palazzo just off Via Maqueda in Palermo, Aurelio Quattrocchi sits writing.

In spring and autumn, a breeze brings in the scent of jasmine and disturbs the loose leaves of paper scattered across the large wooden table at which he sits (he has no desk). A small pile of notebooks sits in a quiet stack at his elbow, only the top one open. In summer, no breeze comes through the open window to stir his papers and the heat wearies him. In winter, the window is closed.

This may not seem an unusual occurrence: Sicily has a fair literary reputation; there are people sitting writing in rooms all across the world. Nor is it unusual that Aurelio writes by hand using a fountain pen with purple ink. Writers are scaramantic creatures, given to rigorously maintained habits.

What is unusual is that Quattrochi has sat in this room writing since he was seventeen years old, and he is now seventy-six. What is more unusual is that in all this time Quattrochi has written only five hundred words.

Speed is an over-rated virtue, especially in literature. Writing takes time; few great works were composed quickly. (Reading, too, takes time: at the *BDLF* we have little enthusiasm for works eagerly described as 'page-turners.' If a writer such as Quattrochi has spent so long putting words onto paper, we should at least pay them the respect of taking their words slowly too, and indulge in the pleasure of well-wrought prose.) Despite this, Quattrochi suffers. He is aware that the slim novel he is working on (*Sulla Lentezza*, an account of the slowly developing friendship between two ageing men set against the backdrop of nineteenth-century agrarian reform) has consumed his entire life.

When he began, as a callow teenager, he foresaw literary glory, not knowing how carefully he would work. Only when he turned twenty-one, having finally completed the opening sentence, did he realise the turn his life had taken.

The seventies were a particularly slow period. He spent all of 1973 poring over a single word, and most of 1974 erasing it. The 1980s, however, saw a comparative rush:

Quattrochi completed an entire paragraph in less than a decade.

If ever asked, which he seldom is, he estimates the work will take until 2042 to finish, a date by which he is aware that he will almost certainly be dead. He has not written a will, but when he does he plans to insist that his manuscript be typed up on the Olivetti Lettera 22 his father had given him as a present when he took his high school diploma.

Nothing changes in his room; little changes outside the window. Quattrochi has seen a small apartment building rise, the jasmine bush become a tree, and heard the sound of traffic grow louder than it was when he began writing. Nothing more.

Slowness is a rare virtue in these times, so we wish Aurelio more of it. We will be patient; we are waiting.

ERIC QUAYNE

OF ALL THE DECEIT, treachery, fraud and outright lies which play an alarmingly large part in the story of literary failure, those of Eric Quayne must surely rank among the most compelling.

Trained as an artist in 1950s London (and the world of fine arts is surely the only one to come close to the literary world for its levels of duplicity), Quayne graduated from the Slade at best only an adequate painter, able to produce reasonable likenesses or pleasing landscapes in the style of whichever painter was currently modish, but found his real skill lay in calligraphy.

Having studied the letters of van Gogh, Gauguin and

Cézanne, he trained himself to mimic their signatures perfectly but their work only badly, thus barring himself from the lucrative profession of pictorial forgery. However, aided by the notorious Louis Nodier (then at his most active in the literary marketplaces of London, Paris and New York), Quayne soon found himself able to escape impecunity by adding to the collected correspondence of a number of great artists. Flush with success and cash, Nodier encouraged Quayne to continue, and soon found himself touting manuscripts of everyone from Voltaire to Dickens to august libraries and university archives from Texas to the Sorbonne. In Soho in the 1960s, Quayne seemed to have found his vocation and became a fixture on that bohemian London scene. Despite his fondness for drink, this may well have been his most fruitful period. Indeed, a number of texts now regarded as canonical in the oeuvres of certain writers whom the *BDLF* shall not name, included in various lists of the hundred books you should read before you die, the reading lists of many chart-topping universities, subjects of earnest Ph.D. theses and BBC costume dramas alike, are actually the work of Eric Quayne.

In the early seventies, Quayne moved to the south of France and, at this point, over-reached himself by completing *The Mystery of Edwin Drood*, producing another batch of poems by Ern Malley, penning Emily Brontë's second novel and writing fragments of Joyce's follow-up to *Finnegans Wake*. Exposure was inevitable, and in a less tolerant age, Quayne's claim to be a tricksy, postmodern experimentalist cut him no slack with severe textual mavens such as Hugh Trevor-Roper (who wrote an exposé in the *Sunday Times* which proved devastating for Quayne).

Undeterred by Melville's maxim that 'it is better to fail in originality than to succeed in imitation,' Quayne moved to Italy and continued to write under his own name, but no one (not even Nodier, by now serving time in La Santé) took any notice of works such as *The Man with the Flowering Hands* or *The Secret Mirror.*

In 1996, Quayne was found dead lying in a gutter in Rome, his head stove in with a blunt instrument. Police claimed he'd died in a drunken fall, then later decided he'd been done in by an angry lover or unpaid rent boy. Other voices do not concur. Who knows how many Eric Quayne had infuriated or shamed with his dazzling acts of mimicry?

HUGH RAFFERTY

⌁ WE HAVE DISCUSSED the dangers of addiction before
on the *BDLF*. As Primo Levi points out in *The Wrench*,
addictions are far from being the exclusive province of
writers, but writers do tend to be prone to them.

Hugh Rafferty (b. Dublin, 1870–d. 1905, St. Giles Workhouse, London) would perhaps today have been diagnosed
with multiple addiction syndrome, but he never saw it quite
like that: he believed he was addicted to nothing but his
own genius. The eighth child of society portrait painter
James Rafferty and light opera singer Henrietta Mulcahy,
Hugh was bundled into a family seething with artistic pre-
tension and large amounts of debt. His father encouraged

the boy to take up smoking at the age of four, believing a pipe to be good for his lungs, while for breakfast his mother insisted he drink what she called 'a little overcoat': a glass of warm milk with a generous tot of whisky.

Despite displaying little natural aptitude, his father insisted he train as a painter, but Hugh soon found his real talent was for verse. Heavily influenced by the Pre-Raphaelites, his first mature composition was *Shadrach, Meshach and Abednego*, a Browningly long piece in blank verse. Rafferty himself called the piece 'allegorical,' yet both contemporary readers (Wilde allegedly kept a copy in his toilet) and critics have not been able to decipher quite what the rambling poem allegorises, and Rafferty himself was always coy about the subject when asked.

He was probably coy because he was drunk. The 'little overcoat' had only been the start. The young Hugh took pints of porter for lunch and at least three bottles of claret with dinner. And this was before he enrolled at art school.

Encouraged by the minor success of his poem, and in-spired by symbolists, decadents, a generous hint of the gothic and various *maudits* (not to mention various day trips to Brighton to visit his friend Eric, who rather charmingly called himself 'Count Stenbock'), Rafferty took to wearing a purple scarf (not particularly decadent, we admit, but he did his best on a limited budget) and soon moved to London in search of a more bohemian life. He frequented Ye Olde Cheshire Cheese, but always man-aged to arrive on evenings when The Rhymers' Club had gathered elsewhere, and consoled himself by drinking as much as he possibly could while reciting his verses to the bar staff. He claimed to compose them spontaneously, but sadly, the next morning he could remember nothing of what he had said the night before.

It was around this period when he inevitably discovered absinthe, and despite not particularly liking it (describing it as 'aniseed ball potcheen'), he decided to dedicate his greatest work ('The Green Fairy') to it. Rafferty would begin writing late at night, having already imbibed enough of the spirit to stun a horse, and scribble furiously for hours until he collapsed at his desk or, more likely, on a bar. Sadly, on waking, he would find that he had written nothing but gibberish.

When the guardians of the St Giles Workhouse (the institute for the destitute where Rafferty inevitably ended up) found hundreds of pages of hastily scribbled verse scattered around his lifeless, wormwood-addled body, they could do little but be baffled, but at least used them to fuel the fire around which they sat drinking port and brandy on the cold evening of the winter day on which Hugh Rafferty's corpse was dumped in an unmarked grave.

LORD FREDERICK RATHOLE

AS WE HAVE HAD CAUSE to point out before, many writers worry about the persistence of their work as much as they worry about its presentation. Sometimes this can even be to the detriment of the work itself. We do not, sadly, have space to discuss the interesting cases of A. Kent Holborn, who spent eight years designing a font which he believed would be the only lexical form dignified enough to contain his work, or that of Maureen Gilhooley, who, despite having a lucrative book deal with a prestigious publishing house, was so insulted by the various cover designs offered her that she refused to go into print altogether.

Let us turn instead to the case of Lord Frederick Rathole (pronounced, as he always insisted, *rath-ole*). This was a mania for preservation of a different degree. Before he had actually composed a word, Lord Frederick decided that his literary output should be preserved for posterity in its own library, a library which he personally would build.

Having rapidly dismissed the services of the finest of architects of his day, Lord Frederick put pen to paper and designed a handsome octagonal building, one side each of which would shelve his works in different genres.

Building work took time to get underway as Lord Frederick arranged to have only the finest Carrara marble and Murano glass imported, then set about trying to find the best craftsmen in the land to help him complete his vision. Once materials and workforce had been amassed, work eventually began only to find that the site on his extensive estate which Lord Frederick had chosen was actually on top of a peat bog, and would not have held much more than a wooden shack. Undeterred, he decided to have an entire wing of his ancestral home demolished in order to provide space for what he saw as being a worthy successor to the great libraries of Nineveh, Pergamon, Alexandria and Constantinople.

Unfortunately, work was further delayed as it turned out that Lord Frederick's blueprints were far from being geometrically accurate, leaving each side of the octagonal building a different length. Lord Frederick dismissed the builders, insisting his vision worked on a higher degree of non-Euclidean geometry.

Twenty-seven years later, his library was complete.

Sadly, during this time, Lord Frederick had been so preoccupied with the building work that he had neglected to write anything. He now spent his time wandering the inside of the admittedly impressive though decidedly curious building, dreaming of the day when those empty shelves would house his great writings.

The library collapsed three years later. Lord Frederick, devastated by the loss, sat down alone one evening, and began to write his only literary legacy. The suicide note ran to a mere three pages, hardly enough to fill a speck of his once-great, empty library.

ROBERT ROBERTS

⌇ IT IS AN UNFASHIONABLE ASSERTION at the moment, perhaps, but there is a theory that writing does have a proleptic quality. That is, an ability not merely to see or predict the future, but to actually *make it happen*. This may date back to the ancient, vocative, incantatory origins of the word and its power over things, to shamanic chanting and oracular sayings, but this kind of vatic strain runs through the history of writing: Blake's visions; Philip K. Dick's hallucinations; Kafka's nightmares; Borges's metaphoric realities; right through to Iain Sinclair's insistence that *Downriver* did not predict the fall of Thatcher, it caused it.

Robert Roberts, perhaps because of the predictive qualities of his very name, the first one anticipating the last,
firmly believed this theory. His first poem was composed
in his early teens and concerned the death of his pet cat,
which had not yet happened. He had imagined the worst
thing that could have happened, put it in writing, and
when, indeed, McWhiskers passed away a year later, Roberts's belief that he had brought the event into being was
formed.

Other things followed: he wrote not with the intention of
causing events, not of predicting but only taking, as many
writers do, what seemed to be the right subject matter to
weave into story or meld into verse. Although his school
was not hit by a neutron bomb, it was closed down six
months after his story 'Disappearance of the Sixth Grade'
was published in a local fanzine (though due to subsi-
dence rather than nuclear threat). As many teenage boys
do, he wrote long poems detailing the agonies of having
been abandoned by lovers whom he had not yet met. (This,
indeed, would happen to him later in life, and on reading
back his old work, he was surprised by the acuity with
which he had managed to predict the events and his feelings, though had not quite calculated the amount of pain
it caused.)

Roberts started to believe not that he was 'a little bit
psychic' as his grandmother had told him, or 'a little
bit psycho' as his rather cruel classmates taunted him, but
that his words had the power to become things.

That writers tend to think of many things at the same time, and that writing does have a scaramantic quality (many write, knowingly or unknowingly, not to excavate or relive trauma, but to confront and ward off their worst fears and failures, and in so doing, overcome them) is true, however. This, we at the *BDLF* believe, is why writing is often an invocation to truth, and an important one at that.

It was not to be so for Robert Roberts, however. Having perhaps overestimated his ability, he wrote a novel, *John Johnson*, about a teenage psychic who went on to become a novelist who won the Booker, the IMPAC, a MacArthur fellowship, then the Nobel (for peace, not literature). Unfortunately, the book was rubbish, and far from achieving its desired results, it has lain in the slush piles of numerous literary agents and publishing houses for many years now, slowly going mouldy, an outcome its author had not foreseen.

BELMONT ROSSITER

SOME WRITERS KNOWN to the *BDLF* occasionally look at the work of E. L. James or Dan Brown and sigh. Not—it should be said—out of dismay at imperfectly rendered prose, poor characterisation and turgid storylines, but out of disgust at the sheer number of digits their sales figures entail. Such writers may even cast their glances at the prestige enjoyed by elder literary statesmen (and they do tend to be men), and seethe internally when thinking of the advances received and cocktail parties attended by Messrs Rushdie, Amis or McEwan.

To assuage their anger and despair, they need think only of Sir Belmont Rossiter.

Belmont Edward George Rossiter was born into the minor aristocracy in 1828, heir to a smart townhouse in

Mayfair, a thriving estate in Hampshire and a not inconsiderable fortune. He published his first work (a book of verse entitled *A Garland of Poesy*) when he was only seventeen, fresh from Eton and about to go up to Cambridge, and the following year's subsequent volume, *Weeds and Wild Flowers*, won the Chancellor's Gold Medal for English Verse. At Trinity, he shifted his attention from poetry to the then-burgeoning novel form, and over the course of his next seventy years published no fewer than fifty-three novels, five collections of tales, several histories, a memoir and four further volumes of poetry.

His success, even at a time when literary men could become national figures, was dazzling. His very first novel, *Henderby of Henderby Hall*, sold out of its initial print run of five hundred copies within a matter of days and was soon being reprinted by every unscrupulous publisher throughout the British Isles.

Rossiter could not be stopped. Each book was more successful than the last. *Cheveley, the Man of Honour* was the highest selling novel of spring 1850, and its successor, *Captain Claridge's Great Mistake*, outsold that fivefold. Literary London was aflutter and working men's associations across the country were set up, helping sheep-shearers and costermongers to read only so they could devour the latest in Rossiter's oeuvre. No genre was safe from his attention: *The House and the Brain* was his foray into horror writing, *The Royalist's Revenge* was a historical novel, *The Coming Race* science fiction and *A Lady of Leicestershire* a tear-stained romance. The colonial settings of the adventure stories

Kenelm Chillingly and *Ernest Maltravers* were among his most wildly successful tales, and were both made into early films (their nitrate film long since turned to ash).

We could list his many other works, but frankly, they are too boring to bother with.

Known as Writing Rossiter to the chronically unimaginative press, he was called Bel by his friends, though he had very few. He challenged Dickens to a duel and allegedly tried to poison Wilkie Collins. Worried by the rising reputation of the Brontë sisters, he once tried to use his rapidly growing fortune to buy up every edition of their work and have them pulped. He told George Eliot she looked like a horse.

Despite, or perhaps because of, his personal failings, Rossiter was offered an army commission and a seat in parliament (both Tories and Whigs were keen to engage his support and services), but turned everything down, preferring to sit in his country retreat and dedicate himself to writing. On his death at the age of eighty-seven from a rare venereal complaint, his fortune was estimated to be enough to buy Hampshire.

But try to find anything of Belmont Rossiter now. Look on the open shelves of your local library, then try the reserve ones. Scan the catalogue of the British Library. Ask an expert on Victorian literature. Trawl through secondhand or antiquarian bookstores in Hay-on-Wye, London, New York, Amsterdam or Paris. Pore over their catalogues. Consult dealers in rare first editions. Try Amazon or AbeBooks, or Google itself. Go on, try.

BENJAMIN RUST

BORN IN 1906 in Headingley, an unexotic suburb of Leeds, to a family that was neither suffocatingly middle class nor intriguingly lower class, Benjamin Rust was a solitary child, much given to bronchial infections and poking around in libraries. Having distant parents, no siblings, and playmates who regarded him as a 'bit odd' from an early age, Benjamin grew up with his imagination as his best friend.

His imagination (which he named Azeroth, after a minor demon he had read of) led him to places which, today, may not seem strange for a teenage boy. (Indeed, were Benjamin alive today he would probably be a successful

MMORPG player.) By the time he was thirteen, he had already read the *Lesser Key of Solomon*, *The Book of Thoth* and the *Smaragdine Table*, as well as a number of other esoteric texts, and this resulted in the disappearance of a number of neighbourhood cats.

As he grew older, Rust joined various orders of the Golden Dawn, lesser Masonic chapters and diverse branches of Theosophists (surprisingly numerous, in Leeds), and decided to document his experiments. Influenced by Arthur Machen, H. P. Lovecraft, Count Eric Stenbock and Algernon Blackwood, he thought that lightly fictionalising his experiments and experiences would bring him greater success and attention.

Indeed, much like J. D. 'Jack' Ffrench,* Rust decided it was not enough to use his few adolescent adventures and a thorough reading of Aleister Crowley as materials for his fiction, and though Azeroth (his imagination, remember) was a fertile creature, Rust decided the thing he needed to do was to summon up a demon for himself, see what happened when he set it loose in suburban Leeds, write down the results and 'hey presto,' one might say (though Rust himself would almost certainly have said something altogether more cabbalistic and complex).

Finding a goat proved rather troublesome, though he did his best, and eventually got one to sit within the pentangle he had carefully chalk-marked on his bedroom floor. He

---

* See entry no. 12.

then went through a number of procedures described in the many arcane demonologies and grimoires he had consulted, and, after the neighbours last saw him hauling a rustled sheep through his front door, Benjamin Rust was never seen again.

His parents found nothing but a scorch mark on the rag rug, though later considered this may have been left by a piece of cheap coal. It was, however, noticeable that all his writings had also disappeared.

We at the *BDLF* do not believe that Benjamin Rust was dragged down into a circle of hell by a low-ranking demon—but writers be warned: when we mess with the written word, we know not what we may bring into being.

CHAD SHEEHAN

BEWARE of first lines.

A great incipit to a poem or story, we are often told, is essential to its eventual success, that striking image or statement an essential hook with which to gather the reader in and keep him or her engaged for the rest of the journey through the work. The opening of a story is a promise which the rest of the tale has to deliver.

Chad Sheehan was first struck by a great opening sentence when he was eighteen years old. Possessed by the perfection of the line that had come unbidden into his head, he went out and bought himself a spiral-bound notebook, carefully inscribed the handful of words and left the rest of the notebook empty, awaiting the moment when a second line would surely follow, tailed by a third then a fourth and so on and so on until the work reached its completion, fulfilling the promise that opening line had made.

This never happened. No sooner had Sheehan written out his great opening line when another one came to him: the perfect beginning to an entirely different story. Sheehan rushed out, bought another notebook, wrote this new first line at the top of the opening page, and then found himself unable to continue. By now he had been possessed by an utterly different idea and its attendant perfect introduction.

The process continued, sometimes rapidly, sometimes more slowly, until Sheehan possessed 1,917 notebooks, all carefully filed in his small apartment, each one awaiting completion.

A new idea has not come to Sheehan for several years now, and despite his insistence on being included here in the *BDLF*, we were initially hesitant, as lack of fulfilment is not yet an achievement of failure. Though we were tempted to reproduce some of Chad Sheehan's great opening lines (many of which are indeed highly impressive), we shall not, and let them rest where they are, a sentinel of warning to those who fear the blank page.

SIMON SIGMAR

THERE IS MUCH to be said for the idea that the literature of the twentieth century is that of memory. From Beckett struggling to forget, to Nabokov urging it to speak, to Borges's Funes tormented by everything he can remember, to Sebald haunted by everything.

Pity, then, Simon Sigmar. Born in Dresden in 1922, Simon was an aspirant poet whose verses were never published due, as he thought, to their decadent qualities and the onset of the Second World War. But this was not his tragedy. Simon avoided being conscripted but found himself interned for being a suspected Communist, then managed somehow to survive the horrors of imprisonment only to be liberated by the Red Army and returned home after a six-week walk to discover his city flattened and burned, his parents missing, presumed dead, and his only surviving sister shocked mute with horror, and pregnant.

Sigmar, then, was a man with much to bear witness to, yet unfortunately found himself living in a city controlled by such repressive apparatus that anything he tried to publish, or even to write, was resolutely suppressed. He soon found himself under close observation, being carefully monitored due to his dangerous tendencies.

Eventually, he tried to escape by concealing himself in a large plastic bag and hiding in the boot of a car travelling west. He made the crossing and survived the journey, but part of his brain did not: on being revived, he was found during the eighteen-hour ordeal to have suffered from some kind of aneurysm, which left him unable to remember anything that had happened longer than ten minutes previously.

He had brought some of his notebooks with him, but now when he read them they made no sense to him. He had the impression that it was a terrible story that had happened to someone else and was relieved that such trauma had not happened to him. A blessing, of sorts.

Despite his loss of long-term memory, Sigmar reported feeling haunted by some kind of sense of loss. He would often spend hours walking around his room looking for something he could not find, though was unable to say what it was that he was searching for.

In some part of his still active mind he knew he had to write, to tell the story of what he could not remember. He had piles of notebooks in which he would begin to write, but by the time he had composed more than a few sentences, he had no idea what or why he was writing or how the last word he had written related to the ones he had begun with. Some shadow of his earlier life would occasionally loom into his mind, but by the time he had found paper and a pen, Sigmar no longer had any memory of the incident he had struggled to recall.

Not even Oliver Sacks, who visited Sigmar in the late 1970s, could help.

If the literature of the twentieth century was all about memory, what role could there have been for Simon Sigmar? He knew everything, and remembered nothing.

ELLEN SPARROW

ONCE CONSIDERED NOTHING but the deranged scribblings of lunatics, the category of 'outsider art' is one that is now formally recognised by the art establishment, however controversial that definition remains. The question that we at the *BDLF* beg to ask, however, is what would 'outsider literature' look like?

To help us answer the question, we can turn to the story of Ellen Sparrow. Born in London, out of wedlock, in 1882, she was placed in an orphanage until a distant aunt appeared when Ellen was nine. (Her aunt, having little or no knowledge of Ellen's father, gave her the surname 'Sparrow,' having seen such a poor creature freeze to death, dropping like a stone from the window ledge of the dormitory young Ellen shared with a dozen other girls.)

Her aunt, it turned out, had a notable interest in spiritualism and theosophy, and young Ellen soon became a fixture at her regular séances. It may have been here, some commentators have suggested, that Sparrow's later peculiarities were engendered.

When Sparrow was thirteen, finding herself alone for the first time in her aunt's East End terrace, she was visited by a spirit which called itself Escribor. And Escribor told her to write.

So Ellen Sparrow, a good child, did as she was bid, and began to write down everything Escribor dictated to her. There being little paper in the house, Sparrow attempted to accomplish her spirit's ardent commands by writing on anything she could find. Old newspapers, bills, receipts of sale and fish wrappers were soon covered in her spiderish writing (she later claimed Escribor had learned her her letters, too). Things came to a head when Sparrow was sixteen, and finding herself with no materials to write on despite her spirit's ever more insistent bidding, she scrawled thousands of words across the walls of her aunt's house, her tiny handwriting only beginning to glean the tale the spirit had told her.

Her aunt took a dim view of this, and had the walls instantly repapered thus losing an early example of Sparrow's work. (The words may still be there somewhere, concealed under layers of wallpaper in some now-fashionable

Dalston or Shoreditch two-up two-down, assuming it survived the Blitz.)

All writers, in one way or another, write to please a
spirit, benign or malignant. But none seemed as insistent
as Ellen Sparrow's Escribor.

Aunt Madge died a year after the wallpaper incident,
and the bereft Sparrow was sent to Hanwell asylum, where
she would stay until 1952. It was during this time that she
composed most of her work.

There, she found the rolls of Izal toilet paper perfectly
suited to her needs, inscribing them with pencil marks
(a pen, with its sharp point, was deemed too dangerous) in handwriting that was too tiny to be deciphered
by the naked eye. The pioneering psychiatrist Max Glatt
attempted to decipher some of them with the aid of a mag-
nifying glass, but even he eventually gave up due to glau-
coma. (Sparrow herself, on the one occasion she was asked,
claimed that she was not able to read what she had written.) Over the fifty or more years she spent in Hanwell, it
is estimated that she covered some ten thousand rolls of
paper with her work.

Other inmates remember her writing at great speed,
muttering or singing to herself as she did so. Then it
would stop, sometimes for months. Sparrow underwent
deep depression during these periods, and voluntarily
underwent sessions of deeply traumatic ECT. Her doctors
hoped it would cure her; Ellen hoped it would bring Escribor back.

She died in 1954, shortly after having been discharged from the asylum, and finding herself living homeless and destitute. The only thing which accompanied her lifeless body was—inevitably—more writing (on rolls of higher-quality paper, at least, taken from the toilets in Victoria station. Unfortunately, these final manuscripts were so soaked by the driving London rain as to fall apart at the first touch. Nothing survives of them).

Had she drawn pictures, Ellen Sparrow would now be remembered in the same breath as Henry Darger or Madge Gill. Sadly, Sparrow had chosen words.

KEVIN STAPLETON

EVEN TAKING INTO ACCOUNT the vagaries of literary fashion, it seems a shame that travel writing is no longer what it was. A field which includes Ibn Battuta and Richard Hakluyt, a Victorian pseud like Richard Burton or a great female voice such as Freya Stark, and reached huge commercial popularity in the 1980s with the no-less slippery Bruce Chatwin, surely deserves more than half a shelf in your local Waterstones or Barnes and Noble.

It may be this age of easy travel and the Internet which has brought about the genre's demise, but try using Dickens's, Twain's or Stevenson's accounts as a guidebook and discover how infinitely richer the experience is than that of trying to use a Google Maps app to find a half-decent restaurant.

Kevin Stapleton, born in Stockport in 1963, was a boy brought up on tales of travellers and wonder. Or, at least, he would have been, had he been fortunate enough to have had good parents and one of those teachers from the movies. Instead, Kevin had only some back issues of *Look and Learn*, a worn copy of a *Children's Illustrated Atlas of the World* and a selection of Willard Price's *Adventure* series.

It was enough. Stapleton grew up with a vivid imagination but few practical talents and, on leaving school at the age of sixteen in the late 1970s, found himself shunted into a YOP scheme and its inevitable successor, the dole.

That great malady of writers, utter penury, limited his opportunities. Stapleton spent his first cheque on a typewriter (a Silver Reed SR 180), thus leaving himself unable to afford even an off-peak day return to Birmingham.

This did not deter Stapleton, and he spent the next few years in his bedsit writing tales of great journeys to Ceylon, Siam and Persia, unaware that those countries had ceased to exist. He sent his work to publishers, who were initially interested, but on finding Stapleton was a twenty-year-old dolehead from Manchester and not some grizzled ex-colonial telling tales from the verandah, they began to return his thick brown envelopes unopened.

(And here we are forced to ask another question: if Stapleton had called his books 'novels', or posited them as postmodern questionings of the genre's assumptions, how successful would they have been? Stapleton was, in a certain way, a victim of that curious and deadly twenty-first-century affectation, a desire for authenticity.)

Hope still clung to him, however, and when after six years Stapleton realised he suffered not only from poverty but also from an acute case of agoraphobia, he was not deterred.

Even though his greatest journeys now consisted of travelling no farther than the shared bathroom in his hallway, or even, on a good day, as far as the Londis minimarket for half a pint of skimmed milk and a loaf of sliced white, he continued to write. His greatest work, *My Day*, concerned the voyage from his bedroom to the toilet, then to the kitchen, where he made himself a cup of tea and some beans on toast, recounting his meetings with the people he found along his route, and was replete with anthropological insight and utter poignancy.

Last we heard, Stapleton had moved into sheltered accommodation near Stretford. One day, Kevin, we shall all read your work, and marvel.

MOLLY STOCK

THE QUESTION OF WHAT OR HOW to write is one which has vexed all writers, though perhaps no less so than the equally serious question of *where* to write. For those fortunate enough, there may be the room of one's own, be it a tiny bedsit or a quiet book-lined study with a view over heritage woodland. Others claim the literary café or even corporate coffee shop is the place, with the buzz of caffeine, the element of *flaneurism*, the free heating. The sofa works fine for some, the kitchen table for others. The options are many: a beach hut, or a cabin in the mountains? A bland Travelodge room, or a five-star hideaway retreat? Alone, or in a room full of people? On the bus going to work? Using a notebook while out walking? In a public library, replete with the background hum of yelling children, mobile phones and half-heard conversations?

Each writer, and each story to be written, requires their own space.

Not unlike many writers, Molly Stock took some time finding her perfect place to write.

After she graduated from Royal Holloway in 1952, her story 'Winter Trees' was published in the student journal *Early Days* and widely read among certain circles. She was talked of as a promising lady writer of the time. Ongoing correspondence with Cyril Connolly encouraged her, but also pointed out that while she was undoubtedly talented, her work still lacked form, substance, assurance, that something which transforms the adequate into the brilliant. This lack, Stock decided, was due not to a deficit of talent, but to not having the perfect writing environment.

She took her notebooks, manuscripts and portable typewriter (a lovely mint-green Hermes Baby) around Lyons Cornerhouses, Soho pubs, Kensington Park and a distant aunt's house in North Yorkshire. But the words did not come.

Then, having trouble rousing herself one cold January morning, Molly Stock found it. She realised she didn't need to bother searching. Here was her perfect writing environment: her bed.

Bed, bed, bed. Bed, lovely bed. Soft and warm and comforting, as big as a house, covers to pull over her head or pillows to prop herself up on. The lovely cool bit hidden at the bottom where she could stretch her legs and wiggle her toes. The cradling divot in the centre, the same shape as herself.

At first she tried placing her typewriter on the bed, but even the delicate Hermes Baby with the support of a tea tray weighed too much, upsetting her perfect equilibrium. So she went back to paper and pen, and other than the occasional dressing gown–wrapped mission to kitchen or toilet, she sat in bed and began to write.

She kept the curtains half drawn, occasionally angling her head to peek out at the gusty or snowy weather beyond, and felt herself safe in bed, writing.

The leaves of paper mounted as thickly as her cotton sheets, woollen blankets and goosedown quilts. Page after page piled up around her, tumbling onto the cold floor.

Eventually trips to the loo or for more tea and crumpets became ever more taxing, and ever fewer. She snoozed, she slept, she snored. The bed was so warm, so soft, after all. Writing was hard; sleeping was easy.

Friends occasionally popped by to visit, and though she assured them she was fine, she soon went from promising lady writer to deluded eccentric.

After she stopped seeing visitors, claiming she was too sleepy or too cosy to open the door to them, Molly Stock's biographical trail sadly disappears. She was last heard of in a boardinghouse in Islington in 1963. We hope she finished her stories, and we wish her sweet dreams.

The strongest writers, of course, could probably write anywhere, in any conditions. Claiming the environment is not right, that the time of day is wrong or that there is too much or too little noise may only be one of the many obfuscatory delaying tactics writers habitually delude themselves with.

But Stock's lesson remains: writers, beware of not only what you write, but also where you write.

PETER TRABZHK

EVERY CITY SHOULD HAVE its own writer. Dublin has Joyce, Prague has Kafka, Buenos Aires belongs to Borges, London to Dickens and New York to, well, take your pick. Some cities, however, sadly remain writerless. Manchester, for example, has tried to lay claim to Anthony Burgess, but with little success or, indeed, motive. Being born in the place is not nearly enough.

There are many cities across the world that remain sadly orphaned.

Take, for instance, the city of Bzyzhzh. A little-known place, neatly but perhaps somewhat uncomfortably nestled on the border between Poland, the Czech Republic and

Germany, the city (it calls itself a city, despite numbering few more than fifty thousand inhabitants) had quietly tried to mind its own business despite a turbulent thousand-year history encompassing countless invasions, several name changes and appurtenance to a number of different countries.

While we pity the city without a writer, we also pity the writer without a city. Such a man was Peter Trabzhk. Trabzhk had been born into a rootless existence, son of an Italian mother and a German father, failed farmers and itinerant agricultural workers in Argentina. Having spent much of his young life travelling that vast country, earning his crust working as a book-keeper, when he was twenty-seven he decided he had earned enough to take a trip back to his motherland, to discover the roots he didn't know he had.

He never found his roots, due to a long story involving an antiquated map and a non-existent command of any of the languages he encountered on his travels. Indeed, quite how he wound up in Bzyzhzh remains obscure. It is possible, we surmise, that he was attracted to the place simply because its complex spelling reminded him of his own orthographically intricate surname.

Regardless, in 1972 he arrived there—unknowingly tailed by spies from four different countries—liked it, and even though he had never written a word before in his life decided to become a writer and write the story of Bzyzhzh.

A complete history would obviously have taken far longer than a young writer wants to wait, so he began judiciously with a series of short poems inspired by Edgar Lee Masters's tedious *Spoon River Anthology*, a copy of which he had picked up while travelling through Italy, where it remains inexplicably popular. The local newspaper was interested and printed a few of them in its 'Poets' Corner,' but there was little wider interest.

He reached out and, this time inspired by *Dubliners* (a Czech copy of which was orally translated for him by a man he met in a bar), wrote a collection of short stories all set in Bzyzhzh, featuring characters he had met during his stay in the city. He was promptly sued for defamation, and all manuscripts were destroyed.

Undaunted, he carried on, and somehow managed to spend several more years in the city, during which time he worked assiduously on what he believed would be his greatest work, a nine-hundred-page epic spanning the whole history of the city. Still feeling uncomfortable with the several languages which jostled for space in Bzyzhzh, Trabzhk's great mistake was perhaps to write the book in his native Spanish, a word of which no one even in the polyglot city actually spoke. Had anyone apart from its author ever been able to read *La ciudad de los tres ríos*, Bzyzhzh may today be on the literary tourist trail. Perhaps, however, it never wanted to be.

HARTMUT TRAUTMANN

HARTMUT TRAUTMANN had long had a passion for the English language. Of the thousands of languages in the world, he felt that only English had such unique variety of inflection, a vast lexis and infinite subtleties of register, all combined with a vigorous directness and utmost grammatical flexibility. What is truly amazing is that Trautmann was able to perceive all this without actually being able to speak a word of the language.

Quite how his particular passion was engendered is unclear. He had been born in East Germany in 1948, so opportunities for learning the language were distinctly limited. Though other linguistic possibilities were presented to him throughout his youth, he found Spanish (promoted in regular visits from Cuban comrades) too in thrall to its Latinate father, Czech and Polish were like having mouthfuls of broken glass, Serbo-Croat didn't know if it was one thing or another and Hungarian was frankly incomprehensible. Russian he refused to countenance. It has been suggested that his love for English was brought about through his enthusiastic devouring of translations of pulp American Wild West novels (Louis L'Amour was strangely popular in the DDR) and a long study of Schlegel's translations of Shakespeare (like many, he believed the two men to be one and indivisible).

He saved money from his job as an electrical engineer and, after ten years on the waiting list, was finally able to purchase a Robotron 202, upon which he set to writing his great novel (in German, hoping to translate it at a later date into English). After several years of work on *Das geheimnis spiegel*, however, Trautmann realised that translation was an inadequate method of expressing himself in English. No, to use the language authentically, he believed, to be able to bathe in its rich resources, to be able to appreciate and manipulate every tiny nuance and shade of meaning, he had to learn to speak the language, to train himself to think in it, and from there to compose directly in the tongue he loved so much.

It was not until 1988 that Trautmann, having carefully used his network of professional contacts to avoid the over-inquisitive eyes of Stasi censors, finally managed to get hold of a German-English dictionary. However, due to the nature of the said professional contacts, the dictionary consisted exclusively of terms particular to the field of East German electrical engineering. Undaunted, Trautmann set out on his task, and beginning with *ampere* and moving through *Gaussian shift* to *orthogonal frequency multiplexing* to *upverting oscillator* and finally to *zener diode* and *zero voltage switching*, he learned English, memorising each and every single term by heart.

It took him seven years to do this, by which time his country no longer existed and English had flooded every advertising hoarding, television channel, instruction booklet and pickle jar label he set his eyes or hands on.

In 1995, having found an antiquarian with replacement parts for the Robotron 202, Trautmann once again sat down to write but found he was unable to string the words he had learnt into any form of meaningful sentence. Always resolute, he continued, eventually making sense of his tale of a frustrated electrical engineer trying to come to grips with a foreign language.

Unfortunately, none of the publishers to whom Trautmann submitted his thousand-page manuscript could make sense of it, and it now remains yellowing, forgotten, in the upstairs room of a tenement block in Friedrichshain, waiting to be rediscovered.

BAS VAN DE BONT

WHILE, POST-DUCHAMP, conceptual art has arguably become the major language of visual arts over the last fifty years, conceptual literature remains much more of a minority interest.

And by 'conceptual literature' here, we do not mean experimental writing, however much we may admire those who cut holes in the pages of their books, wilfully abandon punctuation or engage in wild flights of typographical fancy.

No, here we are talking about the work of someone like Bas van de Bont.

Van de Bont was born in Amsterdam in 1932, and following the war he dropped out of medical school to join *Groep 52*, a Dutch avant-garde collective of artists, poets and pranksters. Though less well-known than some of their European counterparts, the *Groep* 52 were nevertheless influential in establishing notions of the absurd and surreal among their often staid countrymen.

Tired by what he saw as the still-too-restrictive representational practises of stage, screen or page, van de Bont became a founding member of the Situationist International but found himself excluded from that august organisation as early as 1960 for having 'a realist turn' (to quote Guy Debord's oblique communiqué), though more likely it was his growing friendship with the increasingly unstable Jürgen Kittler that led to his expulsion.

During the sixties, he removed himself to an isolated part of Zeeland, and inspired both by Borges and Ray Bradbury set himself to memorising whole swathes of the canon of Dutch literature. This included the early twelfth-century *Central Franconian Rhyming Bible*, the entire oeuvre of Joost van den Vondel, whose tragedy *Gijsbreght van Aemstel* van de Bont saw as having unique relevance to postwar Dutch cultural stasis, and Betje Wolff and Aagje Deken's pioneering 1782 novel, *Sara Burgerhart*. He read with a view of re-creating the whole sweep of his country's glorious, terrible, complex history in a sprawling *Gesamtkunstwerk* the exact proportions and form of which are un-known. (His hut in Zeeland, containing all his notes, was swept away by floods in 1968.)

But it is his work of the early '70s that interests us most. Or, rather, its absence.

In 1972, van de Bont wrote a long letter to his then lover, the French mystic philosopher Catherine Levallois, telling of his newfound passion for the work of Robert Smithson, Marina Abramović, Chris Burden, Joseph Kosuth, the Art & Language group and the Fluxus movement.

The letter delivered, he found a small rowing boat and set off to traverse the entire wrinkled, wriggly, shifting coast of his homeland, armed with only a pair of oars and a typewriter (a portable Adler Tippa S) in what he described as being 'not so much an act as a *gesture* of writing.'

He was never seen again.

'I like art that exists in people's minds more so than it does in reality,' Jeremy Deller has said, and how right he is. How much are we secretly in love with Emily Brontë's second novel, Joyce's 'epic of the sea' follow-up to *Finnegans Wake*, Jodorowsky's *Dune*, Beethoven's Tenth or that Miles Davis–Jimi Hendrix collaboration? How much, while still knowing they'd all probably be disappointments in reality?

At the *BDLF*, we like to think that Bas van de Bont is still out there, somewhere amidst the fogs and floods, rowing and typing. Yet it matters little: what he did not complete is surely as important as what he did.

NO. 44

VERONICA VASS

WRITERS ARE OFTEN secretive creatures, either by instinct or by nurture. The days spent squirreled away in eye-strainingly dark rooms or cloistered libraries, shaping ideas, observations, experiences and rare imaginings into words they can't possibly hope to orally parallel will inevitably form a person given to the pleasures of hiding. At the *BDLF*, we do not hold with those ostentatious flâneurs who sit in cafés or coffee shops, flaunting their MacBooks or Moleskines. Little good will come of it. At the *BDLF*, we have more respect for those who endeavour in silence.

A writer such as Veronica Vass, for example, though we grant that her case is a little extreme. Born in Geneva in

1921 to a Russian émigré mother and a Swiss-Polish father, Vass was one of those women who were presented with a rare window of opportunity by the terrible event of the Second World War. Presciently fearing further convulsions in Europe (though unpresciently fearing Switzerland was to be involved), her family moved to England in 1928. Vass, however, stayed in Brussels, where she was privately educated before coming to Somerville College in 1938. Her formidable intelligence and skill with languages (she spoke five by the age of fifteen, and would eventually add another seven to her repertoire) marked her out as a natural recruit for the secret cryptographic work being carried out at Bletchley Park. (Papers made available recently, however, reveal that her appointment there was not without problems: her mixed European heritage, Jewish father and ironically the very talent with languages that distinguished her also rendered her suspicious in some appointers' eyes. Indeed, it was never entirely clear if Veronica was working as a double, triple or even quadruple agent.)

At Bletchley Park, despite being hidden away in a wooden hut and told not to speak to anyone about anything other than tea dances and buns, Vass met Angus Wilson, Alan Turing and perhaps most significantly the young Christine Brooke-Rose.

Although Vass had already written a novel while at Oxford (the interior monologue *Handflower*, perhaps too heavily influenced by Djuna Barnes to be seriously regarded), it was in the intensely secretive atmosphere of the cryptographic operations centre that her genius for covert work asserted itself.

Over the course of the war years, she wrote five novels, all of them in a code so complex, so treacherous, so arcane that Turing himself couldn't get past the first few words.

Much of the best writing is penetrable only to a certain degree. Who honestly managed to get anywhere with *Finnegans Wake* without several works of reference propped open alongside? Some French-inclined readers would assert that all writing is a kind of code, but none quite as bafflingly impenetrable as the one Veronica Vass used to write her work.

The habit of secrecy inculcated at Bletchley Park ran so deep that many who worked there never spoke about their work even years after the war had ended. So it was with Vass. Not only had she composed her great works in a language for which no Rosetta Stone existed, but then she did not even tell anyone she had written them.

They were discovered by her son following her death in 1979: five typed manuscripts, the ink fading, resolutely refusing to disclose their secrets.

LYSVA VILIKHE

OF ALL THE MANY VARIETIES of failure we have examined so far, the simple, almost banal one of category error has not yet appeared. Yet the simple mistaking of one thing for another, a taxonomic confusion, a lack of understanding about where one thing starts and another ends is one of the most basic and potentially most brutal kinds of failure.

We may, for example, take the case of Lysva Vilikhe, whose book, *A Guide for the Curious Traveller*, could have been one of the greatest novels of the twentieth century, only for people to take it for a poor quality travel guide to a remote and uninteresting city.

A Guide for the Curious Traveller was printed by the State Enterprise for Information and Publishing on poor quality paper, hardly good enough for cigarettes, and bound with cheap glue between badly printed covers in 1959.

Read in one way, the book unsurprisingly gives a number of itineraries for the titular curious traveller to follow around the city, pointing out the monuments, parks, hotels, restaurants and other places of interest in a city remote even for the rest of the citizens of the country in which it is located.

Read differently, however, the book tells not the story of the unnamed city, but rather stories from it: the strange disappearance of the author's father, her mother's sad, slow decline, her adoption by her twin aunts. Then, as she grows older, her own peregrinations around the city in search of its meanings come to the fore, the book almost becoming a crime thriller as the narrator picks out clues to the possible solutions of the many mysteries her life has presented her, finding traces of explanations written into the stones of the streets, the pavements and the buildings themselves.

It is left to the reader to intuit the story of Vilikhe's eventual meeting with a foreign stranger in her city, her brief but passionate romance with him and its sad ending in a station hotel. When implored by her lover to leave with him, she is momentarily tempted to go before turning away, drawn by the possibility of her missing father's return or (reading darkly between the lines) blackmailed by the city's secret services into staying.

If we look at the section *Parks*, for example, we find a description of Yevachev Park, which is described (fairly banally) as having a 'wondrous, romantic view over the river,' and then (more intriguingly) as being 'a perfect place for a secret romantic assignation,' while the description of Kharms Park as a place 'of mystery, where the fun-fair attraction may lead you to lose the one you love' hints at a darker purpose.

If we look at the section on *Hotels*, we find the Hotel Raspberry Bush being 'the best place for an intimate weekend', while the Guest Hotel International Friendship is described as having only one good thing about it: its proximity to the station, and from where, Vilikhe tells us, 'If you are staying here, you will at least know that you are leaving in the morning.' ('If you have to stay there,' she advises us, 'at least stay in Room 22'—the room where her last recorded presence is noted, according to the recently rediscovered State archives.)

Medical Services warns the traveller of the poor quality health provisions, while hinting at her mother's decline and loss. *Bars and Restaurants* tells us where to get some good food, but warns us of falling into bad company among drunks and dissidents.

Why, we are tempted to ask, did Vilikhe tell her story in this fashion, rather than as the otherwise powerful and haunting novel or memoir it could have been? We have no simple answer. Most probably, Vilikhe was attempting to avoid the censors, and therefore told her story in the form of a guidebook rather than in that of the intrinsically suspicious novel. Moreover, she could write directly in English (a language she had picked up in the home of her twin aunts, educated women, included under '*Interpreting and translation services*'), nominally appealing to the wider audience the elders of her city wanted to attract in that brief moment of international thaw. She probably knew no one in her region would read English, least of all the bureaucrats and censors, and even if they did, few would bother with a lowly guidebook for the infrequent visitors to her distant city.

She wanted to tell her story; its container mattered little. Call it a novel, call it a novella, call it a story: it was all the same to her. Call it a guidebook, why not?

The story she needed to tell had taken place entirely in her home city, the city she had never left since birth. (And from which, truth be told, she could not have left, given the restrictions on travel which faced its inhabitants at that time.) We who have lived in the wider world may suppose it was simply her limited horizons that led her to think the smokestacks and concrete apartment blocks, the smell from the mineral processing plant or the unique fall of light on the ever-present snow were among the most beautiful things ever witnessed. But who are we to question her perceptions? Especially when she writes so well of them.

Sadly, in 1961, having decreed the manager of the Guest Hotel International Friendship guilty of ideological impurities, the State Enterprise for Information and Publishing had every copy of *A Guide for the Curious Traveller* located and pulped, despite never having intuited the trenchant, heartbreaking story contained within it.

If we could find a copy of the book, we would follow Vilikhe's every suggestion, even though she describes a city that now has another name, and may well no longer exist.

HERMANN VON ABWÄRTS

THERE IS A THEORY, mooted in some literary circles, that love doesn't exist. This may be putting it too baldly: to put it better, the theory goes that romantic love doesn't exist. Romantic love as we consider it today was, it is said, nothing but a literary formula, a plot device, a formal trope or stylistic invention created by French troubadour poets in the late thirteenth or early fourteenth centuries.

Here at the *BDLF* we naturally find this an intriguing proposition. However (partially due to the state of our research budget and abilities), we have not, sadly, been able to uncover any of these dastardly perpetrators. It would have been fulfilling to find of a certain Guillaume or Hennequin, a Jacquet or an Etienne of somewhere-or-other who had first lusciously described hearts-a-flutter or the sweetness of love's tears, only to find themselves on the receiving end of the real, true, devastating grief that love can cause.

For a look at the phenomenon, we are instead obliged to turn to the case of Hermann von Abwärts. Hermann, born in Kassel in 1770, son of a schoolteacher and a midwife, never excelled at school, being poor at sports and unable to fence. From an early age, however, he did show a marked propensity for writing verse, something which his schoolteachers tried their best to beat out of him.

It didn't work. Hermann composed pages, quires, then reams and sheaves of love poetry, mostly before he was even eighteen years old, and dedicated to a girl he had not met. Not only not met, but who probably didn't exist: all the poems are dedicated to a mysterious 'K' or 'R' or 'M.' A census reveals no trace of any Katerina, Rosa or Margaretha whom he could possibly have known. Von Abwärts, it seems, was rehearsing his complex love life before he had even ever actually been in love.

His habit did not stop. After taking a teaching position in nearby Marburg, von Abwärts fell deeply, passionately in love with the school principal's wife. After being challenged to a duel by the principal (who had found a none-too-ambiguous poem delivered through his wife's bedroom window late one night), von Abwärts fled, apparently burning the cache of poems he had written to *Herrin* Karolina.

He next shows up in Prague in 1802, hot on the trail of the daughter of a German noblewoman (who believed this amorous young man had been courting her rather than her daughter), after which—more poems burned en route—he turns up in Dresden a couple of years later. It was here he would compose what he believed to be his *meisterwerk*.

Having taken up yet another teaching position, he secretly engaged to be married to a young noblewoman of the city. However, on finding out his daughter's intentions, the Baron von Schroffstein was none too pleased about them and tried to have the upstart rascal von Abwärts (despite the aristocratic pretentions of his surname) run out of town, as modern commentators might put it.

This time, von Abwärts decided he would run no more, and threw down the manuscript of the (frankly derivative) *Sorrows of Young Hermann* at his feet, feeling that his murderous pursuers would actually weep and beg pity of him, should they read of the strength of his feelings for Fräulein Katerina.

Unfortunately, the henchmen the Baron had employed were all illiterate, and used the manuscript to beat him thoroughly around the head before he was knifed and thrown into an unmarked grave, his words beside him.

BARON FRIEDRICH
VON SCHOENVORTS

~~THE MORE WIDELY READ amongst us will, no doubt, recognise the name of Baron Friedrich von Schoenvorts as a minor character in one of the lesser-known works of speculative fiction by Edgar Rice Burroughs. This commonly held belief is, however, erroneous.

The real Baron Friedrich was, perhaps unsurprisingly, a nineteenth-century Prussian Junker and himself a prolific writer of speculative fiction, of which, sadly, nothing survives.

The Baron began his writing career in his early twenties. Having married into the noble von Schoenvorts family (his own origins remain unclear, though it is thought he may have been the illegitimate child of a wayward von Schoenvorts uncle and a strapping stable lass), he was soon faced with the intolerable boredom of life on a ramshackle east Elbian estate, and gave himself to the literary muse in order to be able to neglect his other (minimal) duties. His early works, amounting to some ten thousand pages, were in the genre which today would be named 'erotica.' Unfortunately, the formidable Baroness chanced upon her husband's manuscripts and made him take them into the garden and burn them in front of the entire host of the estate's retainers, thus blocking Baron Friedrich's diligent pen for several years.

His name reappears around the turn of the century when he bought himself a commission in the Prussian military (possibly to escape the Baroness's attentions). Though by no means a nautical man, he soon found himself commander of an early U-boat. As he believed the closeted life of a submariner to be the perfect setting in which to write, the Baron installed a typewriter in his small cabin. (The machine in question was thought to be a Sholes and Glidden Remington No. 1, an expensive and extremely heavy import, but was more probably a lighter and more patriotic choice, a Fabig and Barschel Faktotum.)

Underwater, Baron Friedrich found his element. He locked himself in his cabin for days on end, subsisting on a diet of nothing other than plum brandy and charcoal biscuits, writing as though his life depended on it. His sub-aquatic period gave rise not only to a six-volume history of the von Schoenvorts family (insisting, perhaps improbably, that they were descended from one of the lost ten tribes of Israel), but also to an entire series of works dealing with an undersea colony of Martian invaders plotting the downfall of Western civilisation. Said evil-doers were constantly thwarted in their attempts to use the Crown Jewels as the lens for a death ray, turn the Eiffel Tower into a spacecraft or poison sausages by the dashing Baron Heinrich von Vortschoen.

It was on an emergency stop near Biarritz (to collect more paper and typewriter ribbons rather than much-needed fuel) that Baron Friedrich first met the enigmatic Lys La Rue,* who would accompany him and his crew on many of their adventures.

Meanwhile, the First World War had broken out, apparently unbeknownst to the Baron, who saw the constant attacks on his U-boat as nothing other than a distraction at best, an attempt to sabotage his writing career at worst. As a result, the Baron gave command to unhesitatingly blast any craft that approached them as far out of the water as possible.

It was this rash act that gave rise to his fame as a barbarous yet fearless patroller of the Atlantic, and led to him appearing in certain U.S. newspapers where, it is thought, Burroughs may have seen the name during his

---

* Possibly one of the various pseudonyms of Elise La Rue (see entry no. 22).

time as an apprentice to a pencil sharpener salesman in Idaho.

Due to his poor navigational skills, Baron Friedrich believed himself to be somewhere under the North Pole ice sheets when his craft was wrecked on the rocky Azores. He believed he had finally found his magical undersea kingdom, though his crew, by now starving and mutinous, disagreed and summarily shot the Baron through the head. They sent all of his manuscripts to a watery grave when they set light to the remains of the Schoenvort U-boat, and watched it sink below the waves, where, we surmise, it lies to this day.

NATE WARONKER

WE ARE PROVERBIALLY TOLD not to judge a book by its cover, and in the same way we should not judge a book by its girth. Length should never be confused with quality. This obvious fact, however, has not stopped many people from doing so. A cursory glance at any list of the longest novels ever written also includes a notable showing from books many people believe to have been among the greatest ever written. Even short story writers are often not given due credit until they have produced a hefty *Collected Works*.

It was in this spirit that Nate Waronker, a young, eager aspirant from Ohio, fresh out of his MFA, decided not to take the usual route of sending out finely honed short stories to slim literary journals, but instead to aim high straight away and write the longest novel ever written.

This, he was sure, would set him head and shoulders above all his contemporaries who would sit in the library finely honing their prose, sipping mocha lattes from spill-free biodegradable cups while he carved his place in the annals of literary greatness and list sites all over the Internet. Instead of earnestly discussing Raymond Carver and Lydia Davis, Waronker reached for the *Guinness Book of Records* and did some extensive Googling.

He had difficulty setting a bar. The only book he'd actually read and which he'd planned to emulate, David Foster Wallace's *Infinite Jest*, came in a fair lightweight with a mere 484,001 words. (And isn't that extra 'one' intriguing? We wonder if DFW didn't add it on purpose.) *War and Peace* was a contender with nearly 600,000 words, *Atlas Shrugged* (popular with a certain kind of business student on his campus, he had noted) almost equalled it. Waronker was intrigued by Kalki Krishnamurthy's *Ponniyin Selvan*, which tolled a pleasingly round 900,000 words, but couldn't find a copy of it in the library and began to doubt its existence. *Clarissa*—which he was supposed to have read as part of his undergraduate degree but had instead found the Cliff's Notes to be far more manageable—was up there with 984,700 words, but it was *In Search of Lost Time* which regularly came in tops, at some 1,200,000 words.

He had originally planned to read all these great and lengthy works, but having loaded them all onto his Kindle, he didn't feel the pleasing weight of the great tome he wanted to write, so didn't bother, instead opting to sit down and begin the million and a half words (he had set his target) of *The Longest Novel Ever Written* (an arch postmodern wink, or lack of imagination? We leave you to decide).

Waronker was pretty quick with a keyboard, but soon found he had trouble managing more than three thousand words a day, often not achieving half that number. At this rate, he calculated, even resting only one day a week, it would take him more than two years to complete the book. This seemed like an infinity to a young, eager man. Moreover, he came up against the problem that although he knew *how much* he wanted to write, he had little idea precisely *what* he wanted to write.

Last heard of, Nate Waronker was still sitting in a Starbucks on the campus of his Midwestern liberal arts college, having taken to double espressos in an attempt to keep his word rate up. We wish him well.

WENDY WENNING

LEAN, TAUT PROSE. Writing as tight as a bow-string. Refined lexis and stripped-back syntax. These were the things Wendy Wenning liked. Wenning schooled in a creative writing class filled with men who wrote what they knew, knew what they wrote and little else. Stories of upholsterers, French polishers and hardware store clerks with ex-wives and drink problems. No words were wasted in Wenning's workshop. The tutor praised the amount of white space on the page.

Later, Wenning fell for a certain type of broadsheet reviewer. Those for whom every word was essential. She began to mistrust anyone who revelled in language, and threw out the thesaurus her grandfather had given her. Didn't even put it in the recycling bin. She mistrusted puns, avoided alliteration, grew to abhor metaphor. Character development was nothing but cod psychology. In her darker moments, Wenning thought Hemingway too fancy for his own good and found Richard Ford positively baroque. David Foster Wallace made her feel ill. Sometimes she looked amongst the cabbage stalks and coffee grounds in the garbage can, watching her thesaurus rot, not throwing it out but taking grim pleasure in its gradual decay.

Wenning was not without illustrious precedent. She thought of Ezra Pound's razor and red-pen work on *The Waste Land*, or Gordon Lish giving Carver a severe haircut. She wasn't wrong: while restored, integral or unexpurgated editions may proliferate, there is little doubt that Eliot's poem or *What We Talk About When We Talk About Love* would be anywhere near as impressive without such savage editing.

Wenning had been at work on her great novel of postwar American life for years. But then she discovered she had lost control of *An Empty Chair*, and realised what she had to do. She had to kill her babies.

She made some coffee, sat down and began to edit. To refine. To purge. Nouns are our friends, verbs our workhorses, adjectives our enemies. She removed every adjective from her book. Once that task was completed, she turned back to the beginning and started again. Relative clauses went next, then the passive voice. Metaphor, simile, symbol. All felt the knife. None were spared. It was for their own good, she knew. Sometimes she spent an entire day on one sentence or sat up deep into the night trying to find words with fewer syllables. No fat.

She checked her word count every day. The lower it got, the more determined she grew.

She began to think Emily Dickinson bloated, Lydia Davis indulgent. Wenning's style wasn't reticent or domestic, nor did she ever think herself as working with a small canvas. No miniaturist or minimalist, she believed reducing her words to their very essence would release them, to tell a story as huge as its paper consumption was small.

As the months passed, she watched her thousand-page epic become a novella, then a short story. Flash fiction came, went. A prose poem. But still too fat. She wouldn't let anyone see her work until it was perfect.

Then one morning towards dawn after a long, harsh night of black coffee and charcoal cigarettes, she had it. She leaned back, hit the print button, listened to the machine whir, then looked at her masterwork. A perfectly blank sheet of paper.

IVAN YEVACHEV

WHEN IVAN IVANOVICH YEVACHEV finally had a telephone installed, a veil of contentment and pride descended upon him and his mother. He gazed proudly at the black Bakelite apparatus sitting on its own specially appointed table in the kitchen of their small flat on the Arbat and finally felt he had been recognised. Not so much, he thought, for their patriotic fortitude during the difficult period after his father had not returned from the war, but for 'The Widow's Legs,' a short tale published in the journal *Mir* and recipient of 1929's Young Socialist Writers' Prize.

His consequent decisions to join the Writers' Union and

avoid some of the more avant-garde elements of the Moscow coterie of writers, he felt, only bestowed more honour upon him, although the telephone steadfastly refused to ring. He need not worry, other members of the Union assured him, the Comrade himself had read the story, and had greatly appreciated it.

Over the next few years, Yevachev wrote several other works. Although the editors of *Mir* and *Zvezda* turned them down, he was not discouraged and found space in journals whose circulation almost reached double figures in which to share his writings.

When he heard that other writers—some members of the Union, others not—had begun to receive not only telephones but also telephone calls, however, he grew frustrated. He sat for hours in his flat, cooking pots of kasha for himself and his mother, glowering at the silent phone. In 1935, he wrote a story about it, 'The Phone Call,' copied it out longhand (not having been fortunate enough to receive a Moskva typewriter, a fact which may have percolated some amount of envy into the fateful story), and distributed it among some trusted members of the Writers' Union.

The phone call eventually came at 2:15 in the morning of August 29th, 1935. Having waited many years for this moment, Yevachev hurried himself out of bed and picked up the receiver with a mixture of hope and anxiety.

'Good evening, Iosif Vissarionovich,' he said, amazed to hear the words finally coming from his own mouth.

As far as we know, Ivan Ivanovich Yevachev never wrote again.

Nor did he ever receive another telephone call. The next night there was merely a large black car pulling itself up outside their apartment in the middle of the night, two men the size and shape of wardrobes knocking quietly on the door.

His only published story, 'The Widow's Legs', was removed from all extant copies of the journal in which it had appeared, and Yevachev's name expunged from the roll of prize recipients.

Wherever Yevachev went in that car or on the train that may or may not have followed it, we like to believe that as he travelled he was thinking of Chekhov on his way out to Sakhalin, or Dostoevsky heading for Omsk, not knowing they would one day return to write their greatest works.

At the *BDLF*, we are hesitant to call this 'failure,' for in many ways it is an act of great heroism. Following some editorial debate, we have decided to include him, if only to remind ourselves that he is not alone.

WILSON YOUNG

TRAVEL IS A RAW MATERIAL of the mind that every writer should have.

Some, indeed, would have it up there in the well-worn pantheon alongside show-don't-tell, murder-your-babies, application-of-bum-to-seat and so on: *travel*. Travel brings the useful knowledge, however scant, of a second or third language. It brings the awareness, be it intimate or sketchy, of how people in cultures and climes very different to one's own may negotiate the everyday. In the worst cases, it can at least provide an exotic backdrop to an otherwise dull story. Most important, however, travel can give the experience and feeling of being an outsider, of not being one of the crowd, of being someone *other*. This is perhaps the most difficult thing to achieve, and to acknowledge.

It was this that Wilson Young was obscurely seeking when, having graduated from an English midlands red-brick university at the dog-end of the sorry 1980s and having little direction other than not wanting to become a jobseeker, he decided to travel. To be fair, he did have a vague idea of becoming a writer, but naïvely (like many, let it be said) he thought this was a process that would some-how *happen* rather than one that had to be actively brought about. Travel, he was sure, would help his flowering into literary greatness.

Having little idea where he actually wanted to go, he took a pin, closed his eyes and stuck it into the tatty world map his flatmate used to cover the holes in the wall. Unfor-tunately, the pin stuck in the middle of the Pacific Ocean, the nearest landmass to it the tiny island of Nauru, one of the remotest spots on the face of the earth. Wilson's perilous finances did not allow him to undertake such an adventurous journey at that point, so he began more mod-estly, and went to Paris: a good enough place for a writer to start, surely?

It was less than a week before he was fed up with over-priced arrogance and bad food, so Young headed to the Gare de Lyon and jumped on a train whose destination he did not know.

It was the beginning of a journey that would take more than twenty years, and have no end.

Knowledge is nothing but a map of ignorance, and this Young found out the practical way: the more he travelled, the less he realised he knew. The farther he went, the farther he realised there was still to go.

His ambitions to write changed from vague ideas to stuffed notebooks. He felt he had to tell the entire fascinating and complex history of the town of Bzyzhzh and the tiny, brief country of Cimbria. He had to recount the whole Crimean war, but then realised all this was not necessary: it had been done before, elsewhere, better. He scratched everything, but saved just those few, telling details, the nuance or feeling that would make a work of fiction come alive.

Young filled his notebooks with long, tender, mouthwatering descriptions of the menemen eaten in Istanbul, the manoushi in Beirut and the grilled milza in Palermo, but then realised he was writing a guidebook for gastronomes, not a work of fiction. He recast everything, thinking how his characters may have relished the same food.

He wrote dialogues in the languages he had learned, feeling very pleased with himself but then realising they would probably be incomprehensible to most readers, or at least need a good deal of clumsy exegesis. He scrapped them, or used one telling word to suggest a conversation in a different tongue.

Yet despite all this judicious self-editing, the quantity of material Young amassed during his travels was enormous: Ukrainian folktales roughly translated by a drunk in a bar in Lvov, a story of a Portuguese settler in Madras recounted by a taxi driver in an *idli* restaurant in Chennai, ghost stories from a *fattucchiera* on a rancid backstreet in Naples, descriptions of the huge storks he had seen wheeling across the sky in Rabat, the colour of the twilight sea in Kovalam or the bright morning one in Lampedusa. He saw a woman building a house of stones in Palestine, he saw a boy with a pet wolf in Siberia, he saw a girl in the windswept east of England save the life of a baby chick as it struggled across the road then couldn't get up a steep grass verge, and she took it, and held it, and placed it in safety.

All this, he felt, needed to be recorded, and needed to be told. And yet: the travelling, he knew, could never stop. There was still that thought that one day he might get to Nauru.

So he carried on moving and he carried on writing, a writer at last, even though he could form none of his millions of notes into any shape because he had not yet finished travelling. Only when the journey had ended could he write the first word of the story.

He's still out there somewhere. If you come across him, tell him to keep going.

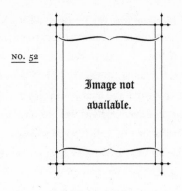

Image not available.

SARA
ZEELEN-LEVALLOIS

ALL WRITING has loss at its heart; all books are records of disappearances.

Throughout this book we have traced many of them, some profound, others less so. While we have occasionally had cause to mock the pompous, we have also tried to remember the true, the talented and the lost.

We will end with the story of Sara Zeelen-Levallois: a writer so dangerously and frustratingly obscure she has challenged even the standards of the *BDLF*.

Her name has only ever been heard in whispers, eavesdropped from conversations between people scarcely less obscure than herself. It is possible that she was the daugh-

ter or granddaughter of Eric Levallois (Casimir Adamowitz-Kostrowicki's friend and faithful confidante*), or the
sister of Bas van de Bont's one-time lover,† but no one
knows with any certainty where she was born, grew up,
studied, or even less what ever happened to her.

None of her works have survived, or have ever been seen.
They exist purely in the domain of hearsay and rumour.

She may never have existed at all, or perhaps she is still
alive, out there somewhere, writing.

Those who claim to know her, or know of her, have
talked of poems whose syntax and diction twist language
into new shapes, forming tiny bright daggers sharp enough
to pierce the heart. Others have spoken of a novel so com-
pendious and yet so precise it would change our thinking
about the form, the last true revolutionary work, a thing
that would turn lives inside out after only its first page.
Some have claimed she wrote short stories, brief tales that
twist and turn, things that would checkmate Chekhov,
carve Carver into pieces. Stories that need but a few brief
pages to reconfigure your soul.

The ephemeral, evanescent, scarcely believable career of
Sara Zeelen-Levallois shows us, if nothing else, one important, terrible thing: words will change nothing. Write
how we may, the arrogant and corrupt will still run the

---

* See entry no. 1, also author of *The Girl with the Avant-Garde Face*.

† See entry no. 43.

world, people will starve needlessly, your lover will still leave you.

And yet.

The power of writing is one of the greatest things we have, whether it is read or not. Let her story represent all those who have borne witness and desired their memory to last. Let it be for those who have wanted to leave a mark, a trace, of whatever kind, however slight, on this earth. Let it be for all those who have wanted to say *I was there, I saw*. Let it be for all those who were enchanted and wanted to enchant, for all those who have tried to hold a thought, an image, a memory in a handful of words. Let it be for all those whose lives and work have come to nothing. Let it be for all the lives we could live, of all the people we will never know, the people we never will be, of everything we have had and couldn't keep. This is what the world is, and this is what she wrote of.

At the very beginning of this Dictionary, we asked you to think of 'those dozens or hundreds or thousands whose work has been lost to fire or flood, to early death, to loss, to theft or to the censor's pyre.' We asked you to think on 'what has been lost that could have bettered us all.' At the end, we ask you again.

Memorials, it has been said, are good only for those still living: it is useless to remember the dead or the lost because they cannot remember us. But in remembering them, we give them and their words life. So let us remember.

ACKNOWLEDGEMENTS

MANY have asked how the *BDLF* came about. This is a good question, and merits a good answer. It is, however, a complex story, and sadly lack of space and certain legal niceties prevent us from divulging the whole history of the genesis of the *BDLF*.

Suffice to say that the editor, long preoccupied with the question of literary failure, began to find tantalising traces of untold stories and hidden histories in his long searches of dusty secondhand bookstores, junk shops and flea markets. His constant questioning led to contacts being made and a small group of similar obsessives formed. The story continues with the discovery of abandoned manuscripts in house clearances, trawls through the rotting slush piles of minor literary agents, overheard literary gossip and tales from the failing memories of librarians, book dealers, academics and fellow writers across the world.

The editor would like to thank the dedicated team of biographers and researchers who made this ambitious project possible.

— ACKNOWLEDGEMENTS —

G. B. Shorter (poet, philosopher and barman), Tat Usher (goat expert and delver into basements), Emilie Reinhold (our Franco-Scandinavian agent), the late Eric Levallois (well-connected author of *The Girl with the Avant-Garde Face*), Bethany Settle (library sleuth), Sarah Mount (book addict), the ever-unreliable Fausto Squattrinato, Jonathan 'Johnnycakes' Kemp (forager into the dark underbelly of the Great Wen), Madame Holette (rock 'n' roll rambler through the British hinterlands), and K, wherever she is now.

C.D.R.

INDEX

C. D. Rose was born in the north of England and studied in several of that country's elite universities, including the University of East Anglia, where he went to do an M.A. in creative writing, and Edge Hill University, where he is at work on a Ph.D. His research into great lost literary works drew him on to live and work in several different countries, including Italy, France, Russia and the United States, where he enjoyed a number of encounters with curious authorial personalities. His research interests have not abated, and now, though based in England, he continues to travel in an unending quest for that one elusive, perfect tale.

Andrew Gallix is the editor in chief of *3:AM Magazine*. He writes fiction and criticism, and teaches at the Sorbonne. He divides his time between Scylla and Charybdis.